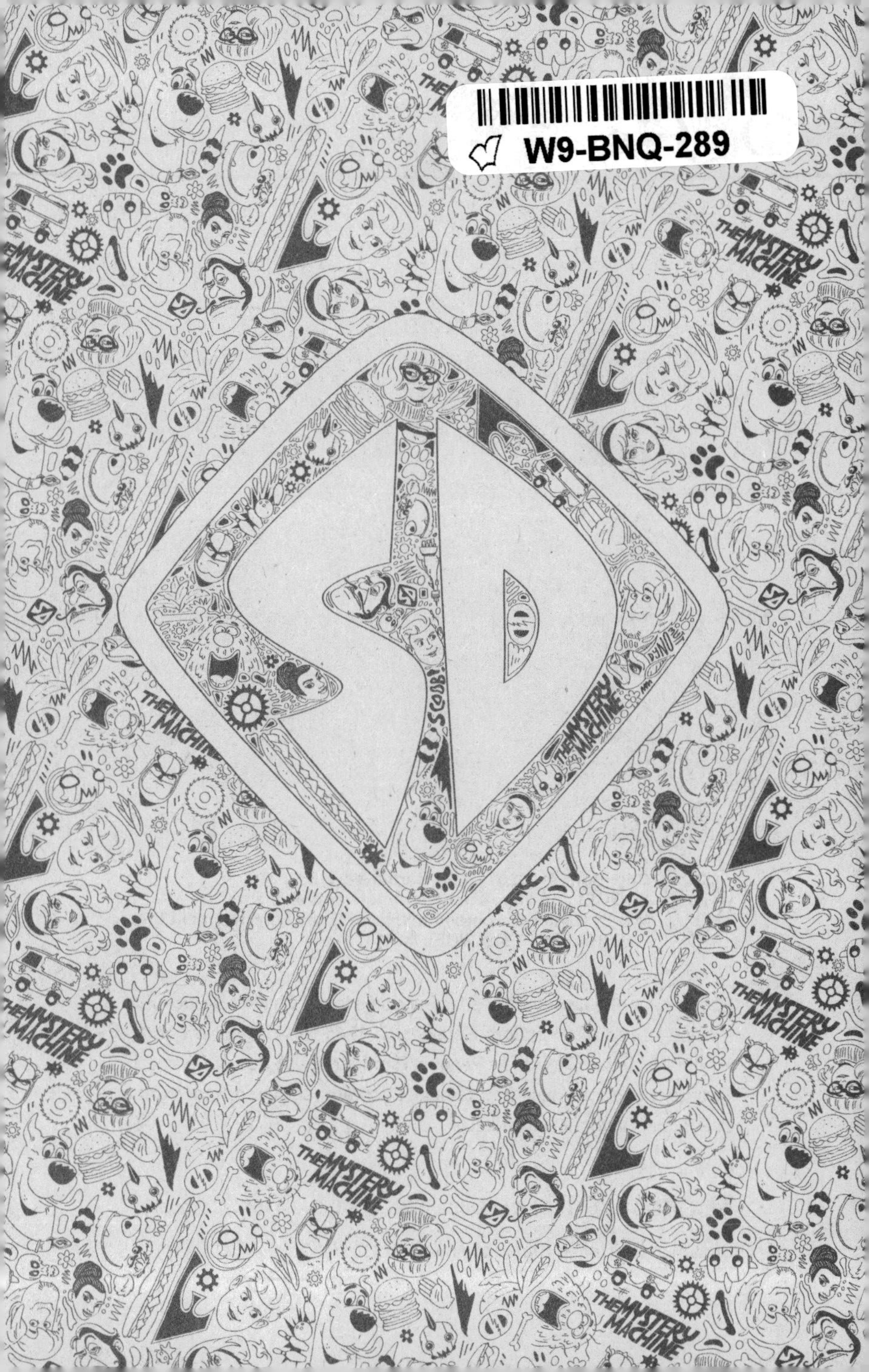

Published in the United States by Random House Children's Books, a
division of Penguin Random House LLC, 1745 Broadway, New York,
NY 10019, and in Canada by Penguin Random House Canada Limited,
Toronto. Random House and the colophon are registered trademarks
of Penguin Random House LLC.

rhcbooks.com

ISBN 978-0-593-17854-6 (pbk.) — ISBN 978-0-593-17871-3 (ebook)

Printed in the United States of America

10 9 8 7 6 5 4 3 2 1

The Junior Novelization

Adapted by David Lewman

Based on the feature film *SCOOB!*

Story by Matt Lieberman and Eyal Podell & Jonathon E. Stewart

Screenplay by Adam Sztykiel and Jack C. Donaldson
& Derek Elliott and Matt Lieberman

Based on characters created by Hanna-Barbera Productions

Random House 🏠 New York

CHAPTER ONE

One beautiful sunny day at the beach, people were riding bikes, playing basketball, and flying kites in the ocean breeze. On the boardwalk, delicious Greek food was being sold at a stand called Alexander's Great Gyros. The smell of the soft pita bread filled with hot meat wafted through the air, mixing with the salty scent of the sea.

SNIFF! SNIFF! A hungry puppy poked his nose up over the edge of the counter at the stand, smelling the tempting food. It was too much for the little Great Dane to resist. He slid his paws across the counter and nabbed a whole big tube of gyro meat!

"Hey!" the owner shouted. "You mangy mutt!"

"Yikes!" the brown puppy yelped. He took off,

rolling on top of the tube of meat, which was almost as big as he was.

"Come back here!" the owner called, chasing after the dog. He gave up when he realized he couldn't serve the meat now that it had rolled across the dirty boardwalk.

Teetering as he tried to keep his balance, the dog rolled along the crowded boardwalk on the meat tube, almost knocking people over.

"'Scuse me!" he called. "Pardon me!"

WHAM! The dog rolled into a park bench and fell off the tube. He watched helplessly as the meat rolled straight into the ocean and sank. *BLORP!*

REE-OOO! REEE-OOO! Blasting his siren, a cop on a bike rode up to a group of sunbathers.

"Did anyone see a stray dog roll by on a tube of compressed meat?" he asked.

"Ruh-roh!" the dog said to himself, sneaking under the bench and hiding behind a backpack. The backpack belonged to a shaggy-haired kid who had just tried to join a game of basketball but failed miserably. The kid reached down and picked up his backpack, revealing the puppy. The kid ambled away.

The bike cop spotted the dog. "Aha!" he cried. "There you are!"

The dog ran off and dove into a pile of sand. He got sand in his mouth and spat it out. *Ptooey!*

He heard a voice nearby. "I'm sure glad I found you guys. I was starting to think I would never have any friends."

Peeking out of the sandpile, the dog saw the shaggy-haired kid sitting on a blanket.

"Today's gonna be a great day!" the boy said.

But he wasn't talking to anyone. He'd sculpted some pretend friends out of sand, giving them seashells for eyes and seaweed for hair.

"At least until the tide comes in," the kid continued. He was holding a sandwich.

The dog spotted the sandwich. He crept over and popped up from behind one of the sand friends.

"AHH!" the kid yelled, startled.

"AHH!" the dog yelled, also startled.

But when he saw it was just a little dog, not much more than a puppy, the kid offered the dog half of his sandwich. The dog took a step back.

"Yeah," the kid said, nodding. "I get it. Nobody likes my sandwiches."

SNIFF! SNIFF!

"Is that liverwurst?" the dog asked, coming a step closer.

"Why, yes, it is!" the kid confirmed. He was amazed and impressed that the puppy could talk. "But, like, I gotta warn you: it's also got sour cream, cucumber, and dill."

"Did you put sauerkraut on it?" the dog asked, cocking his head.

"Of course," the kid answered, looking a little offended. "I'm not a *monster*. Sauerkraut gives the sandwich that—"

"Umami!" the dog and the kid said at the same time.

"Exactly!" the kid said, impressed that the dog knew about umami, a Japanese word that meant "deliciousness" but was also the name of a fifth taste distinct from sweet, sour, salty, and bitter. They laughed, happy to have found each other. They bit into their halves of the sandwich . . . and loved it! Yum!

They smiled at each other, instant friends. But their happy moment was interrupted by the angry bike cop yelling, "Hold it!"

"AHH!" the dog screamed, jumping into the kid's arms.

"This mangy stray has done enough damage for today," the cop announced. "He's coming with me."

"Wait, what?" the kid protested, thinking fast. "He's not a stray!"

The cop frowned, puzzled. He was sure this was the stray dog described by the guy at Alexander's Great Gyros. "Is he your dog?" he asked suspiciously.

The kid made a quick decision. "He's, like, totally mine." Then he whispered into the dog's ear, "If you wanna be."

"I'd like that very much," the dog whispered back.

But the bike cop wasn't convinced. "Okay, then," he said slowly. "What's his name?"

CHAPTER TWO

The kid shot the dog a quick questioning look. "I don't have one," the dog whispered.

"His name is . . . ," the kid began, trying to come up with a good one. He looked down and saw a package by his feet. The box read SCOOBY SNACKS

"Snacks!"

"Huh?" the bike cop said. He'd never heard of a dog named Snacks.

"Snacks?" the dog asked, puzzled.

"Uh," the kid said, thinking, "I mean . . . Scooby!"

"Middle name?" the cop quizzed.

"Dooby?" the kid answered.

"Last name?" the cop asked.

6

"Doo," the kid said.

The cop just stared at him for a moment. The dog chewed his lower lip. Would the cop believe that his name was really Scooby Dooby Doo?

"All right, then," the cop said, turning away. "If the dog's yours, he's off the hook." He rode away on his bike.

"Woo-hoo!" Scooby and the kid cheered.

"I'm Norville," the kid said, "but everyone calls me Shaggy."

"Well," the dog said, "I guess I'm . . . Scooby-Doo?"

Shaggy grinned. "Don't worry," he assured his new friend. "That name will never stick."

🐾 🐾 🐾 🐾

That night, Shaggy gave Scooby a tour of his room. "This is my jelly bean dispenser," he said, pointing to it. "You can help yourself."

"Cool!" Scooby said, picking up the dispenser as soon as Shaggy moved on and pouring all the jelly beans into his mouth.

"And this is my ventriloquist's dummy. I don't really use him anymore, so now he just sits there and gives me nightmares," Shaggy said.

"Scary," Scooby said, shuddering. He pointed to the bed. "Ooh, what's this?"

"It's a bed," Shaggy explained. "You sleep in it."

Scooby climbed into the bed. Then he jumped around, giggling. "Soft! I've never had a bed before. Well, I guess I've never had *anything* before."

Grinning, Shaggy dug something out of his pocket. "Well, you've got something now! I ran out this afternoon and bought you a surprise." He opened his hand, revealing a collar with a diamond-shaped tag that had the initials S.D. on it.

Scooby picked up the collar and examined the tag. Then he put it on. "I love it! I'll never take it off." The new best friends hugged.

🐾 🐾 🐾 🐾

That Halloween, Shaggy and Scooby went trick-or-treating dressed as their two favorite comic book characters, Blue Falcon and Dynomutt. By the end of the evening, Shaggy's pillowcase was stuffed with treats!

"Woo-hoo!" Shaggy crowed. "This is awesome. We hit almost every house in the neighborhood!"

Scooby pointed at an old, scary-looking home.

"What about that house, Raggy?" Whenever Scooby tried to say his friend's name, it came out "Raggy."

Shaggy looked where Scooby was pointing and shuddered. "No way, bro! That's the Rigby house. It's haunted. Like, let's get out of here!" They turned and ran.

But they hadn't gotten very far when Chad and Chet, two bullies on skateboards, grabbed Shaggy's pillowcase full of candy and tossed it through a window of the Rigby house!

"Ruh-roh!" Scooby said.

Laughing, the bullies shoved Shaggy to the ground. Then a voice said, "I think that's enough."

The voice belonged to a strong-looking kid named Fred, who was wearing a knight costume. He was with his two friends, Velma and Daphne. Velma wore a black robe and carried a gavel, while Daphne was dressed as Wonder Woman.

"Whatever," Chad said, pretending not to be afraid of Fred. He turned to his fellow bully. "Come on, man. I'm bored of this anyway."

Chet agreed. They quickly rode off on their skateboards, laughing.

"Are you guys all right?" Fred asked Shaggy and Scooby.

"Yeah," Shaggy said. "They just hurt my pride. And my tailbone."

"Let me give you a hand," Fred offered, pulling Shaggy back up to his feet. "I'm Fred. This is Velma."

"Hi," Velma said, giving a little wave with her gavel.

"And that's Daphne," Fred said.

"Hey," Daphne greeted.

"I'm Shaggy, and this is Scooby-Doo."

"Nice to meet you," Scooby said. He licked Daphne's face. She giggled.

"Cool Wonder Woman costume," Shaggy told her. He turned to Velma. "And are you . . . Harry Potter?"

"I'm Ruth Bader Ginsburg," she explained. "Obviously."

"Huh," Shaggy said, not recognizing the name of the Supreme Court judge. "Is she a wizard?"

"She *is* a wizard," Velma said, nodding. "A wizard of justice."

Fred put his arm around Shaggy. "Come on," he said. "Let's go get your candy back."

CHAPTER THREE

"B-but those jerks tossed it into the Rigby house!" Shaggy sputtered. "It's haunted by a demon ghost!"

"Demon ghost?" Scooby cried, instantly scared.

Velma looked at the big, dark house. "I think the five of us can handle one silly ghost."

"Ghost or no ghost, it's Halloween!" Daphne said. "No one should go home without their candy." She had to drag Shaggy and Scooby along the sidewalk toward the spooky house.

"Uh, okay," Shaggy said. "We'll go in the haunted house this one time. But we're not gonna make a habit of this. Right, Scoob?"

"Right!" Scooby strongly agreed.

On the porch, Fred knocked.

KNOCK! KNOCK! KNOCK!

Nothing.

He slowly reached toward the doorknob. *CREEEAAAK!* The door swung open, and the gang stepped into the ancient, dusty house, which was filled with cobwebs, scuffed antiques, rickety furniture, and creepy statues. As the gang crept inside, Shaggy and Scooby held on to each other for dear life. With every pop and creak of the old floorboards, their heads swiveled and their eyes darted. They expected to see a demon ghost any second!

"Jinkies," Velma said, creeped out.

"This living room feels more like a dying room," Daphne said.

"Hello?" Fred called out. "Mr. Rigby?"

"Anybody home?" Daphne added, her voice echoing through the big house.

Fred spotted the pillowcase full of candy on the floor. He picked it up and tossed it to Shaggy. "Here you are, Shaggy."

As soon as he had the pillowcase, Shaggy headed toward the front door with Scooby.

"Great!" he said. "Thanks a bunch! Let's go!"

As the others began to follow them out—
BANG!
They heard a crash behind them! They stopped and turned around, trying to see what had made the loud noise.

"Ruh-roh!" Scooby said, worried.

"It's the ghost!" Shaggy and Scooby said at the same time.

"Guys, there's no such thing as ghosts," Velma said firmly.

Daphne turned on her cell phone's flashlight and shined it around the room, stopping on a tall wooden cabinet. A beam of light flashed from between the cabinet's two doors! "Did you guys see that?" Daphne asked.

Her intelligent eyes sparkling, Velma slowly walked toward the cabinet. "Hmm . . ."

"Uh, I don't think this is a good idea," Shaggy warned.

But Velma kept moving toward the cabinet. She reached her hand toward the knob and opened it, revealing . . . a row of coats. "Huh," she said, disappointed. She pushed the coats aside and walked into the cabinet, curious to see what was in there.

"Guys," she called from inside. "Check this out!"

The others followed her into the piece of old furniture. Shaggy and Scooby were the last to go in. They shared a look, encouraging each other to be brave. Then they stepped in.

The cabinet was a secret entrance to a storage room full of TVs, game consoles, computers, and appliances.

Daphne spotted a shelf full of designer bags and gasped. "These purses are really expensive! My mom says I can choose between one of these and going to college!"

Velma raised her finger and started to speak, but Daphne cut her off.

"Don't worry. I'll choose college," Daphne said.

Shaggy started to pull out a brand-new computer tablet, still in the box. "No way! Scooby, look at thi—"

"Do. Not. Touch." Velma warned him. "Shoo!" She waved him away from the stack of tablets. "I have a feeling we've just stumbled upon some illegal activity."

Fred opened a box full of watches. "Guys, I have a feeling we've just stumbled upon some illegal activity."

14

"Thanks, Fred," Velma said dryly.

ROOOOAAAAR!

They all spun around and saw a giant demon ghost towering over them!

"ZOINKS!" Shaggy yelped as Scooby leapt into his arms.

"DEMON GHOST!" they screamed together.

The ghost lunged forward, flying toward the gang with its claws out. "RAAAHHH!"

They jumped out of the way and scrambled back through the cabinet. *WHAM!* They slammed the door shut behind them and struggled to shove the cabinet in front of it.

"Daphne! Velma!" Fred yelled. "Get to the door! We'll try to hold the cabinet!"

As Velma and Daphne ran toward the front door . . . *BAM!* The door and all the windows in the house slammed shut, locking them in! They pulled on the front door but couldn't open it.

SCRRRAPE! The cabinet suddenly jerked forward. The demon ghost escaped from the cabinet and crawled across the ceiling. Then the ghost swooped down, knocking the friends to the floor.

"Guys, we gotta *do* something!" Fred shouted.

Shaggy and Scooby knew what to do: they jumped into a big pot and hid under a plant. Fred, Velma, and Daphne started to run upstairs.

But Daphne tripped! She picked herself up and started to run again—and then she saw the demon ghost right in front of her, blocking her way.

"WHOA!" Daphne yelled.

CHAPTER FOUR

"Run, Daphne!" Velma urged. "Run!"

"ROOAAARRR!" the ghost bellowed as it chased Daphne back down the stairs.

Velma looked up and noticed something: a rope dangling from a pulley attached to the ceiling! Whenever the ghost moved, the rope moved.

"Fred, look!" Velma called out, pointing. As the ghost closed in on Daphne, Fred grabbed an axe off the wall and threw it at the rope. *SNAP!* The blade cut the rope!

"Uh-oh," the demon ghost said.

THUD! The ghost fell to the floor on its face. Daphne grabbed the rope, which she now saw had been tied around the ghost's waist the whole time, and held it tight. "Velma!" she shouted.

"Got it!" Velma said, instantly understanding what her friend had in mind. She raced down the stairs and grabbed another piece of rope. Daphne and Velma ran around and around the ghost, tying it up until it couldn't move.

Fred hopped over the banister, grabbing a helmet off a suit of armor. He donned the helmet for safety and tackled the ghost. "Gotcha!" he said.

Thinking it was safe to come out of hiding, Shaggy and Scooby climbed out of the pot. But they accidentally knocked the pot over. *CRASH!* Startled, Scooby jumped into Shaggy's arms.

"AAAHHHH!" they both screamed.

Looking at the tackled figure on the floor, Daphne noticed that the demon ghost was wearing something rubber over its face.

"Jeepers!" she said. "It's a Halloween mask!" She reached down to yank off the mask, revealing . . .

"Mr. Rigby!" they all said at the same time.

"You brats are pretty darn brave," Mr. Rigby admitted.

Though she didn't like being called a brat, Velma smiled. "I think we figured out what's going on inside your 'haunted house'!" she said.

Daphne held up her cell phone, showing Mr. Rigby the screen. "And I've been live-streaming the whole thing. All these thumbs-down and poop emojis tell me you're going to jail!"

URRRREEEE! They all heard sirens as blue and red lights shone through the windows.

A few minutes later, the kids and Scooby watched as the sheriff snapped handcuffs on Rigby and led him toward a police car parked outside.

"Ha!" Rigby barked, looking back at the gang. "I would've gotten away with this if it weren't for you meddling kids!"

The sheriff put Rigby in the back of his car and shut the door.

The police car took off with its siren blaring. *URRREEE-OOO! REEEE-OOOO!*

"Congratulations, everyone!" Velma said. "We just proved this house wasn't haunted *and* busted a perp."

"Perp?" Scooby asked.

"Perpetrator," Fred explained.

"And most of all," Shaggy added, "I got my candy back!" He held up his bulging pillowcase.

"Not bad for a bunch of kids," Daphne said.

Fred grinned. "Maybe we should do this again."

Shaggy looked confused. "Like, trick-or-treat together every year?"

"No, Shaggy," Fred said. "Solve mysteries."

"I like it," Velma said.

"I'm in," Daphne agreed.

Fred turned to Shaggy and Scooby. "What do you say, guys? If we're gonna do this, we're gonna do it together."

"Let's do it!" Scooby said enthusiastically.

"We're in!" he and Shaggy said together.

At that moment, the five of them became Mystery Inc.!

Ten years later, the members of Mystery Inc. sat around a table in a diner. Grown up by then, the team had caught ghosts, mummies, vampires, monsters, aliens, phantoms, robots, cavemen, witches, werewolves, and zombies—usually exposing them as humans in disguise.

"All right, gang," Fred said. "We're all here to solve our greatest mystery yet. What's next for Mystery Inc.?"

"Oh, I totally have the answer," Shaggy said. "Lunch!"

"To figure out what our next move is," Velma said, "I invited an expert to help us. There he is!"

A man wearing a suit and carrying a laptop computer entered the diner. Velma waved, and he walked toward their table.

"Like, who's this guy?" Shaggy asked.

"A team-building expert," Daphne explained. "We hired him to do an analysis of Mystery Inc."

After joining them at the table and opening his laptop, the expert got right down to business.

"I've watched hours of tape on your little mystery gang. I know you better than you know yourselves." He pointed at Fred. "He's your tank, your muscle."

"Cool," Fred said, proud to be described that way.

Next, the expert pointed at Daphne. "Daphne's your people person."

"Aww . . . ," Daphne said humbly.

"Velma's got the smarts and technical savvy," he continued. Then he looked at Scooby and Shaggy. "And you two . . . aren't even listening! You're eating a clownishly oversized sandwich!"

It was true. The two pals were munching on opposite ends of an enormous hoagie. Shaggy swallowed. "Sorry, man. You were saying?"

"Numbers don't lie," the expert said firmly. "I've crunched the data, and I fail to find anything tangible that Chin Whiskers or Talking Dog contribute to Mystery Inc."

Shaggy and Scooby looked stunned. Scooby turned to Shaggy.

"He's mean," he said.

CHAPTER FIVE

Shaggy glared at Fred, Velma, and Daphne. "This feels like an ambush," he said.

"You didn't respond to the email!" Fred protested.

"I can't remember my password!" Shaggy claimed.

"I don't even have thumbs!" Scooby pointed out, though he didn't seem to be having any trouble holding the big sandwich.

Daphne felt bad about the expert's blunt comments. "Shaggy and Scooby are our best friends." Fred and Velma nodded in agreement.

"Ah, yes—friendship," the expert said, wrinkling his nose, as if someone had waved a dirty sock in front of it. "You know why they call it friend*ship*? Because ships sink!" He closed his laptop. "Now, if you'll excuse me, I have many more feelings to hurt in the name of good business." He got up and left the diner.

Shaggy and Scooby noticed that Fred, Velma, and Daphne were staring at them, concerned.

"Listen," Shaggy said. "You're not actually going to listen to that guy, are you?"

"Well," Velma admitted, "he *is* a highly respected expert in organizational efficiency. . . ."

"I don't respect him," Scooby announced.

"We don't need this, Scoob," Shaggy said, feeling hurt and angry. "Let's bounce." He stood up.

"Yeah," Scooby agreed. "We know when we're not wanted." He clambered out of the booth and followed Shaggy for a step or two. He hurried back. "No fries for you," he said, taking his fries.

Then Shaggy and Scooby were gone.

Fred, Velma, and Daphne looked at each other, guiltily.

"Ugh," Daphne groaned. "I feel terrible. I don't think I can work right now."

"That's okay," Velma said, patting her shoulder. "It's not like there's some super villain out there preparing to destroy the world."

🐾 🐾 🐾 🐾

KABOOM! Lightning flashed in the clouds over Machu Picchu, the ancient ruins of an Incan city in Peru. Two archaeologists wearing ponchos and carrying flashlights made their way down stone steps into the site of a dig.

"This is really it," Carla, the first archaeologist, said excitedly. "We've found him."

"Oh, don't tease me, Carla," the second archaeologist, Dr. Fitzhume, said warily. "You've gotten my hopes up before."

"I think it's better if I *show* you," she answered. At the bottom of the stairs, they passed through a door that led to a large ancient chamber. *FWOOM.* Carla switched on a generator, lighting up the room. A massive skull, as big as a truck, sat on a platform in the center of the chamber. Dr. Fitzhume couldn't believe his eyes!

"Oh . . . wow," the scientist said, staring at the gigantic skull. "And you're sure it's one of his?" He leaned in for a closer look, examining the mouth.

"Oh, absolutely," Carla said confidently. "This is unlike the skull of any known species, living or extinct."

"And these teeth," said Dr. Fitzhume, carefully touching the long, sharp fangs. "Woof."

"They're distinctly canine," Carla said, pointing out their similarity to a dog's teeth. "After all our years of searching, we finally found . . ."

"Cerberus," Dr. Fitzhume said, nodding slowly. "The guard dog to the underworld." He walked over to a mural on the wall that showed a giant three-headed dog standing in front of a pile of treasure, baring its teeth.

Carla shuddered. "This is why I'm more of a cat person. How do you think one of the skulls ended up here in Peru?"

"Look here," Dr. Fitzhume replied, pointing at another mural of three skulls on the decks of ships. "These murals show us everything we need to know. The skulls were hidden across the globe in three mystical places. If they were ever reunited, they would have to power to open the gates to the underworld."

Looking puzzled, Carla asked, "Why would anyone want to do that?"

"Because beyond those gates lies a lost treasure," Dr. Fitzhume explained. "Once I have the key to open them, I will be the wealthiest man in history!" A touch of greedy madness shone in the archaeologist's eyes.

Carla was taken aback. "Doctor, is this why you wanted to find the skulls?"

Dr. Fitzhume smiled a thin smile. "You have to admit, unimaginable wealth is a lot more interesting than archaeology." He pulled out a sprayer and aimed it at Carla. "And now I no longer have any use for you."

"Dr. Fitzhume!" Carla gasped. "Why are you being so, so . . ."

"Dastardly?" he said. "Because that's just who I am!" He pulled off a mask, revealing his true face . . . the face of the villain Dick Dastardly! *ZHWOMP!* He sprayed Carla with sticky goo, trapping her against the stone wall. Then he pointed upward and a tarp slid away, revealing the night sky. He thrust his arm in the air, ready to be lifted up. "Now let's claim our prize and go!"

An adorable baby robot known as the Leader Rotten toddled into the room.

Dastardly thrust his arm in the air. "I said . . . let's go!"

But nothing happened. "BEEP BOOP GA-RONK?" the little golden robot asked.

"Of course I mean you!" Dastardly snapped. "Do you think I'm talking to her?"

Intrigued, the robot walked over to Carla and

peered at her. "Help me," Carla pleaded. The robot looked sympathetic.

Dastardly saw this. "Toughen up!" he ordered. "We're the bad guys, remember?"

The Leader Rotten transformed into a robotic scorpion. *"HISSSS!"* Carla drew back, terrified.

"Now stop messing around, you metallic miscreant!" Dastardly yelled at the robot. Punching a button on his watch, the villain signaled the *Mean Machine*, his massive airship. A giant claw descended from the ship and grabbed the skull, lifting it into the sky. Dastardly and the Leader Rotten jumped onto the skull and climbed into the claw as it rose.

FWOOOOM! A bright beam of light shone from the skull and swept the dark sky.

"Good doggy!" Dastardly said, patting the skull. "Show me where your brothers are hiding!"

He flipped open his watch, revealing a small screen. The skull's beam of light locked on a location, and GPS coordinates flashed on the screen. "Excellent!" Dastardly hissed. "We've got it!"

He looked down at Carla and grinned an evil grin. "Toodle-oo!"

CHAPTER SIX

Carla couldn't believe what she was seeing. The huge skull rose slowly into the night sky and flew toward the ominous airship. "Blue Falcon will stop you!" she cried.

"Let him try!" Dastardly scoffed. "I'm the early bird this time. It's my turn to get the worm!" He and the Leader Rotten rode the claw up into the hull of the *Mean Machine*.

When they were inside, the Leader Rotten jumped off and transformed back into a baby robot.

"Listen up, you gold-plated pipsqueak," Dastardly barked. "The skulls are useless to me without the key. I'm trusting you to proceed to Phase Two: Operation Gimme Paw."

The Leader Rotten chirped, saluted, and ran off to carry out his master's orders.

🐾 🐾 🐾 🐾

WHOOOM. Inside a bowling alley, Scooby held a paw over the hand dryer, getting ready to bowl. Shaggy pushed French fries around in a basket, brooding.

"You believe the nerve of that expert dude?" he asked. "He doesn't think we contribute to Mystery Inc.!"

Scooby picked up a bowling ball and held it to his chin, staring down the lane at the ten pins standing at the end. "What does he know?" he said to Shaggy. He launched the bowling ball. As it rolled, he leaned left, hoping to get it to hit the perfect spot on the front pin. *WHACK!* Pins went flying. Nine fell, but one remained standing.

Shaggy stirred the little paper cup of ketchup with a fry. "Yeah, you're right," he said. "If the other team members don't appreciate us, then who needs 'em?"

"Good point, Raggy!"

"As long as we have each other, we'll be just fine on our own."

"Right!"

Scooby grabbed his ball from the automatic return and rolled it down the lane. *KLOK!* It knocked down the tenth pin! "Yes!" Scooby cheered.

But then the pin popped back up into place! Scooby shook his head in disbelief. When he stared down at the pin, he saw it had two little red eyes! "Eyes!" Scooby said. "Raggy, look!"

Shaggy turned to look. The eyes were gone. "Huh?" he said.

"The pin!" Scooby insisted. "It has eyes!"

The metal bar came down and swept the pins away. Shaggy touched Scooby's shoulder, but his friend jumped, rattled by the sight of the red eyes on the bowling pin. "Oh, Scoob," Shaggy said sympathetically. "I know it feels like everyone's judging us today. Even the bowling pins. But don't freak out on me, bud."

Shaggy walked over to the ball return to get his ball and take his turn. His ball wasn't there. He peered into the hole the balls popped out of and saw nothing. He pressed the ball-return button. Nothing happened. Confused, Shaggy kept pressing the button. "Uhh . . ."

"What's the holdup?" Scooby asked.

"The ball return won't return our ball," Shaggy explained.

Balls were popping out of the returns at the other lanes, but not Scooby and Shaggy's. Finally—*SHWOOMP!*—their ball reappeared.

"Oh!" Scooby said, relieved. "There it is."

Shaggy reached for the ball, but it tried to bite him! He yanked his hand away. "Zoinks!" he cried. Then *all* the balls and pins transformed into Rottens, looking like scorpions with metal fangs, green eyes, and Taser tails! "Like, what is going on?"

"What are those things?" Scooby asked.

"I don't know," Shaggy said, "but they don't look friendly."

He was right. Moving as a coordinated pack, the Rottens attacked! "Look out!" Shaggy shouted.

"Doh!" Scooby yelped.

"This way!" Shaggy said, running.

With the Rottens in close pursuit, Shaggy and Scooby ran past a bowling alley employee named Judy.

Too busy staring at her phone to notice the chaos around her, she said, "No running."

Thinking fast, Scooby and Shaggy dove over the counter of the snack bar, taking cover.

"What now?" Scooby asked.

"Follow my lead," Shaggy said.

They popped back up, dressed as snack-bar workers.

"Who's hungry?" Shaggy asked. Two of the Rottens eagerly approached the counter.

Scooby handed them menus, and they immediately forgot all about their mission. "Check out the specials!" Scooby suggested.

"So, like, what are you guys in the mood to eat?" Shaggy asked in his friendliest voice. "And please don't say 'human.'"

"Or 'dog,'" Scooby added.

The first Rotten beeped and booped. Shaggy jotted down his order. "Okay, Bowling Alley Yakitori." He looked at the other Rottens. "And how about you guys? Hot wings to share?"

Menus in hand, the other Rottens started beeping out their orders.

"BEEP!"

"BOOP!"

"BEEP-BEEP!"

"Got it," Shaggy said, scribbling on his pad. He looked at a Rotten who was still studying the menu, considering every item. "And for you?"

"BOOP BEEP BOP BEEP-A-BARP-A," the Rotten said, ordering.

"Oh, no!" Shaggy cried. "We're out of calamari!"

The Rotten was instantly furious, ripping the menu to shreds. The other Rottens destroyed their menus, too.

"AAAHHH!" Scooby and Shaggy screamed as they darted away.

Over by the shoe-rental counter, a Rotten jumped up and stole Judy's phone.

"AHH!" Judy shrieked, instantly furious. "DIE!" She grabbed a bowling ball and smashed the Rotten. Unfortunately for her, she also smashed her phone.

Scooby and Shaggy ran back toward the bowling lanes with a swarm of Rottens flying right behind them.

"This way, Scoob!" Shaggy yelled. He dove into one of the lanes, sliding along the waxed surface with Scooby right behind him.

"AHHHHH!" they screamed again.

CHAPTER SEVEN

CRASH! Shaggy and Scooby slid through the pins and slammed into the back wall of the bowling alley. *WHAM!* After they landed in a pile of boxes, Scooby spat a bowling pin out of his mouth.

Shaggy sat up and looked around. "I always wondered what was back here."

"Underwhelming," Scooby observed.

🐾 🐾 🐾 🐾

At that moment, Fred, Daphne, and Velma were patrolling the streets in their van, the Mystery Machine, listening to a police scanner for leads on criminal activity.

"All units," crackled a voice from the scanner. "Attention, all units. We have a four-one-five in progress at the bowling alley."

Velma flipped through a police manual to see what a 415 was. "Here it is: 'Attack by tiny, violent, shape-shifting robots.'" She looked up from the manual. "Wow, the police really do have a code for everything."

"The bowling alley?" Daphne said, sounding concerned. "That's where Scooby and Shaggy hang out!"

"Oh, no!" Fred said. "Let's go!" He turned the steering wheel and hit the gas, heading for the bowling alley. *ZOOOM!*

🐾 🐾 🐾 🐾

Just then, Shaggy and Scooby ran out of the bowling alley and into the dark passageway behind the building, slamming the big metal door behind them. *CLANG!*

"Did we lose them?" Scooby asked.

BANG! BANG! BANG! The Rottens were hammering on the other side of the door!

"Pretty sure we didn't," Shaggy answered.

BANG! BANG! BANG! With each pound, another Rotten-shaped dent appeared in the metal. And with each dent, Scooby and Shaggy screamed, moving to avoid the bumps in the door. They ran down the alley, right into a . . . dead end! When they looked back, the Rottens were cutting through the door with lasers.

"Yikes!" the two pals screeched.

The Rottens burst through the cut door, pouring into the alley. Trapped, Scooby and Shaggy held on to each other, trembling.

"Looks like this is goodbye, old buddy," Shaggy said.

Just as the Rottens were about to reach them— *PHWOOOM!* A blue tractor beam blazed down on Shaggy and Scooby. The Rottens backed away, shielding their eyes from the dazzling light.

"AAHHH!" Scooby and Shaggy screamed as the beam lifted them into the air.

🐾 🐾 🐾 🐾

THUD! Scooby and Shaggy landed on a hard floor. Shaggy helped his friend to his feet.

"You okay, Scooby-Doo?" he asked.

"Yeah," Scooby said. "I'm good. Where are we?"

They looked around. Lights snapped on, one by one, illuminating an empty blue room. Then Shaggy recognized an emblem on the wall.

"Dude. Hang on. Do you realize where we are?" he said.

"No," said Scooby, shaking his head.

Shaggy opened his arms wide. "Look around, man. The clean, modern aesthetic. The cool blue color palette. We're in . . ."

Scooby stared at Shaggy expectantly.

". . . the *Falcon Fury*!" Shaggy exclaimed.

ZOOSH. A panel slid open and a woman in a high-tech uniform stepped out.

"Gentlemen, welcome aboard," she said. "I'm Dee Dee Skyes, pilot of the *Falcon Fury*."

"Well, we're—" Shaggy started to say.

"Scooby and Shaggy," Dee Dee interrupted. "We know. Follow me." She turned and started walking briskly. Shaggy and Scooby could barely keep up as they followed her down a long, brightly lit hallway.

"Who sent those robots?" Scooby asked.

"I bet it was that team-building expert!" Shaggy said. "So mean!"

Dee Dee kept walking. "No, it's actually this guy named Dick Dastardly. He's trying to kill you."

"Scoob!" Shaggy said. "Somebody thinks we're important enough to kill!"

"It's nice to be wanted," Scooby said as he and Shaggy high-fived.

At the end of the hall, Dee Dee opened a door and led them into the *Falcon Fury*'s atrium, a super-high-tech control center where crew members operated holographic displays. As they walked through the room, Shaggy and Scooby couldn't believe what they were seeing.

"I know it's super cool in here," Dee Dee acknowledged, "and I would totally let you guys press random buttons, but they told me we need to move."

Suddenly—*ZWOOM!* The ship went dark!

"Now? Seriously?" Dee Dee said, annoyed. "We're doing this now?"

"Is it him?" Shaggy asked. "Is it him?"

"Yes," Dee Dee sighed. "He likes to make an entrance."

Smoke started to fill the room. A voice came over a speaker: "Ladies and gentlemen! Since the dawn of time, the falcon has been worshipped as a symbol of freedom and victory. Now a *new* kind of falcon rules the sky. And he is one bad mamma jamma. . . ."

"BLUE FALCON!" Shaggy and Scooby cried.

Music played! Spotlights swung around the room! Lasers lit up the fog!

"DJ BLUE FALCON!" the voice announced.

A hole opened in the floor. A silhouetted figure began to rise on a platform. . . .

CHAPTER EIGHT

The figure was big: tall, with broad shoulders and thick muscles.

Blue Falcon.

Shaggy and Scooby's eyes couldn't open any wider.

"Welcome to the *Falcon Fury*," Blue Falcon said in a deep voice. Then he looked up, puzzled. "Hang on, hang on. Turn on the lights!"

The lights snapped back on.

"Where are my balloons, Dee Dee?" Blue Falcon complained. "When I say '*Falcon Fury*,' that's the cue for the balloons." He called to the unseen announcer: "Keith? What is the deal up there, man?"

The voice came over the speakers. "I missed the cue."

"Duh," Blue Falcon said. "You've got one job, pal."

Dee Dee couldn't believe this discussion was even taking place. "I'm sorry I had to decide between Keith being in charge of missile defense and your balloon thing. . . ."

Blue Falcon turned to her, shocked. "The balloon 'thing' is important, too. Okay, Dee Dee? And I do not appreciate the 'tude." Then he remembered he had guests, and turned to Shaggy and Scooby. "Anyway, welcome aboard. I'm Blue Falcon."

"No, you're not," Scooby said.

"Yes, I am," Blue Falcon insisted.

"I told you I wasn't going to be the only one who noticed," Dee Dee said.

Shaggy pointed at Blue Falcon's uniform. "No, Blue Falcon's suit has a bigger red *F* on the chest, and it's way less scaly."

Blue Falcon looked at his chest. "Those aren't scales! They're feathers! It's called an upgrade! This ain't your daddy's Blue Falcon."

A voice came from behind Blue Falcon. "In this

case, it most certainly is not."

Dynomutt stepped into view. "Allow me to introduce you to Blue Falcon's large, adult son, Brian."

"Dynomutt!" Shaggy and Scooby exclaimed.

"Oh, *him,* you recognize," Blue Falcon groused.

"Well, sure, man!" Shaggy enthused. "Dynomutt is the dog wonder!" Scooby pinched Shaggy. "Ow!" he yelped. "What was that for?"

"Making sure this isn't a dream," Scooby said, thrilled to meet his hero.

Shaggy pinched Scooby back. "You're supposed to pinch yourself!"

"Ow!" Scooby cried. They pinched each other, back and forth, until Dee Dee cleared her throat.

"Ahem! Finished?" she asked.

Scooby got in one last pinch.

"Ow!" Shaggy cried.

"Finished?" Dee Dee repeated.

"Yes," Scooby said.

"Wait," Shaggy said, realizing what Dynomutt had said. "Brian, if—"

"Blue Falcon," Brian corrected him.

"If you're Blue Falcon now," Shaggy asked,

"does that mean . . . ?"

"Yes," Brian said, nodding. "Regretfully, my father has moved on to a better place."

"Oh, no," Shaggy said sadly.

"What? Oh. No, no," Blue Falcon said, realizing Shaggy had misunderstood him. "He's not dead. He retired to Palm Beach."

BWAAAT! BWAAAT! A warning blasted through the ship.

"Huh?" Blue Falcon said as the lighting shifted to "red alert."

Dee Dee checked a hologram. "Oh, no! It's Dastardly!"

"Let's move on!" Blue Falcon said, leading the way into the *Falcon Fury*'s cockpit.

Shaggy and Scooby ran after them. "Like, hey, wait up!" Shaggy called.

In the cockpit, Blue Falcon ordered Dee Dee to take the helm. She hopped into a Gyro-Pod and grabbed the controls. A holographic display floated in front of her.

SHOOMP! Seats shot up under Blue Falcon, Shaggy, and Scooby and buckled them in.

"Punch it, Dee Dee!" Blue Falcon commanded.

"Engaging oscillation over-thruster!" Dee Dee responded.

Inside the *Mean Machine*, Dastardly hit an accelerator, jerking his Rottens back as the airship shot forward.

"Hang on!" Dee Dee shouted, zooming the *Falcon Fury* ahead. It swerved around the *Mean Machine*, cutting it off.

"What's Dastardly's deal, anyway?" Scooby asked.

Blue Falcon turned to him. "The rumor on my fan site is that Dastardly's collecting the three skulls of Seabiscuit."

"That's Cerberus, Brian," Dynomutt corrected him, bringing up a hologram of the three huge dog skulls. "Right now he's got one skull and needs two more. Try to keep up. If Dastardly opens the gates, we're talking total annihilation."

"Annihilation?" Shaggy asked.

"End-of-the-world stuff," Blue Falcon explained. "You know the drill."

"We so do not know this drill," Shaggy admitted.

In the *Mean Machine*, Dastardly glared at the *Falcon Fury* as it rocketed upward. He followed, hot on its trail. "Hold tight!" He shoved the throttle forward, sending the Rottens tumbling around the cabin again.

In the *Falcon Fury*, Scooby and Shaggy were terrified. Dee Dee tried to maneuver the ship. "I can't shake him!" she cried.

From his command chair, Dastardly ordered, "All right, Rottens! Launch the harpoons!"

CHAPTER NINE

SHZHOOOOMP! Harpoons with cables attached to them shot toward the *Falcon Fury*. Dee Dee tried to dodge them, but the big ship wasn't fast enough, and several harpoons pierced it.

"What is going on?" Shaggy shouted.

"Oh, no!" Dee Dee cried. "Dastardly's pulling us in!"

Towed by the cables, the *Falcon Fury* was moving closer and closer to the *Mean Machine*.

"Dynomutt!" Dee Dee called. "Can you reverse the polarity of our tractor beam?"

Dynomutt scanned a control panel. "I think so, but that would mean it would be a repulsion. . . ."

"Exactly," Dee Dee confirmed. "Reverse on my mark."

"On it!" Dynomutt said.

Dee Dee rotated the *Falcon Fury* so it directly faced the villain's ship.

In the *Mean Machine*, Dastardly shot a confused look at his Rottens. "What's happening? Why have we stopped pulling in that ship?"

Back in the *Falcon Fury*, Dee Dee shouted, "Now!" Dynomutt smacked a panel, and the ship's tractor beam blazed straight at the *Mean Machine*, blinding Dastardly.

The villain cried, "Oh, no, no, no!" as the *Falcon Fury* lurched backward, pulling free of the harpoons.

As their ship spun out of control, Shaggy and Scooby were thrown around the cockpit, their faces distorted by the force.

"AAAAHHHH!" they cried.

Dee Dee managed to get the *Falcon Fury* upright and sped away. "Are you guys all okay?" she called.

"Like, if you want, you can pull over and drop us off here," said Shaggy. He'd had enough. "We'll walk home."

"We'll walk home," Scooby echoed.

Later, Shaggy and Scooby followed Blue Falcon and Dynomutt down the ship's main hall.

"Until we figure out what Dastardly wants with you," Dynomutt said, "I think it'd be safer if you joined us on our mission."

"It would?" Scooby said doubtfully.

"Ring-ring! Ring-ring! Ring-ring!" Blue Falcon said. He pretended to answer a phone. "Hello? Uh-huh? Uh-huh. Yeah, of course." He turned to Scooby and Shaggy. "Uh, guys, it's adventure calling. And it's for you!"

Shaggy pretended to take the phone from Blue Falcon. "Hello, adventure? Yes, will you take my name and number off your list?" As he started to hand the pretend phone back, Scooby took him aside.

"But, Raggy," Scooby protested. "It's Blue Falcon! Sorta."

"Yeah, true . . . ," Shaggy admitted. "And, like, I guess joining this team would show our old team what they're missing." He and Scooby looked at each other, then turned to Blue Falcon and said, "We're in!"

"That's what I'm talking about!" Blue Falcon said, clapping them on the back. "Now, I've got a couple of waivers for you guys to sign. . . ."

Just then, a hundred balloons fell from the ceiling.

"Oh, great," Blue Falcon said. "Great timing, Keith!"

"Sorry, B.F.!" Keith said over the speakers.

At the bowling alley, Fred, Velma, and Daphne found out from Judy that Shaggy and Scooby had been there but they'd left.

"What happened?" Fred asked.

"I don't know," Judy said. "They seemed pretty bummed out. I guess their friends dumped them in a coldhearted way or something. And then this blue light came down from the sky and beamed them up."

"Whoa, whoa," Fred said. "Shaggy and Scooby were *taken*?"

"Yeah," Judy said. "I'd have to assume that if they were with their friends, they wouldn't have been kidnapped."

Daphne, overcome with guilt and concern, gasped, "I can't breathe!"

"Whoever these 'friends' are must be carrying a ton of guilt on their shoulders right about now," Judy went on.

Velma held her hands up. "Okay, can you skip the emotional punishment and describe the robots, please?"

"Yeah, sure," Judy said. "They look like what's in this box." She pulled it out to show them. Inside was the Rotten she'd smashed with a bowling ball.

Fred, Velma, and Daphne peered into the box. "Whoa," they said.

Judy let them take the broken robot with them. Back in the Mystery Machine, Velma inspected the damaged Rotten.

"Guys, this thing is incredible," she said. "It's fully autonomous and capable of modifying its external appearance. I'd like to shake the hand of whoever created this!"

Fred and Daphne looked puzzled. Velma noticed, and said, "And then, you know, throw that hand in prison for trying to kill our friends. Right? Am I right?"

Daphne leaned in to take a closer look at the mangled robot . . . and spotted something!

CHAPTER TEN

"Ew," Daphne said. "Is that a hair?"

Velma plucked a single black hair from one of the robot's joints. "Maybe this can lead us to our culprit." She held the hair up to the light.

"What are you doing?" Fred said, grossed out. "Touching it with your fingers?"

"Grow up, Fred," Velma said. "Do you know how many stray hairs the average human eats every day without knowing it?"

"If it's more than zero, I don't want to know," Fred said.

Velma put the hair into a high-tech device. It analyzed the hair and showed the results on a screen. "Huh," she said. "Traces of mustache oil. Soil particles with a mix of arsenic, selenium, and . . . sunblock?"

She went to her computer and typed in the results. "Let's see if the combination of these elements matches a geographical location." A match popped up. "Bingo!" Velma said. She zoomed in on the location and read aloud, "'Dastardly Demolition'?" She quickly typed "Dastardly Demolition" into her computer. "Per county records, the last known owner is . . . this guy." An image of Dick Dastardly appeared on the screen. "Dick Dastardly," she said. "And he's got a long criminal record!"

"Let's go get him!" Daphne said.

Fred hit the gas, and the Mystery Machine peeled out. The broken Rotten slid to the back of the van . . . and its eyes blinked open!

🐾 🐾 🐾 🐾

Meanwhile, up in the *Mean Machine*, Dick Dastardly was addressing his Rottens with the help of his main Rotten lieutenant, the Leader Rotten.

"So," Dastardly said, "was Operation Gimme Paw a failure? Yes."

"CHEEP!" the Leader Rotten chirped.

Dastardly whirled on him. "I'm talking! Of

course it was a failure, because you failed me. You are responsible for my suffering."

The lieutenant chirped sadly. "BLEEP BLORPY."

"Oh, sorry? You're sorry?" Dastardly said, leaning down and nodding. "You certainly are. And I thought my *last* sidekick was worthless! At least he had a backbone, with fur and a wet nose. But you. You've lowered the bar to new depths of craven ineptitude I didn't even think were possible!"

Thinking this was praise, the Leader Rotten puffed out his chest and beeped.

"That's not a compliment, you aluminum imbecile!" Dastardly bellowed. "You're not a partner. You're a disgrace, a lemming, a boot-licking suck-up." He spotted a handheld vacuum cleaner. "An example must be made!"

He popped off the robot's head and chucked it into an incinerator. "If you're going to be a sniveling suckface, you might as well look the part!" He jammed the small vacuum cleaner onto the Rotten's body. Then he turned to the other Rottens.

"Forget you mechanical morons! I'll fetch the key myself. It's time for Dastardly to take his rightful place: center stage!"

On the *Falcon Fury,* Dee Dee and Dynomutt scanned a hologram of Earth, searching for likely locations for the skulls. Blue Falcon stared at his phone.

"To find the second skull," Dee Dee explained, "I'm searching every location with high fossil density."

"Brian!" Dynomutt barked. "Quit putting filters on your selfies and get in the game!"

Blue Falcon looked up from his phone. "Whoa, whoa. What do you think I'm doing? I'm putting my social media feelers out there, Dynobutt."

Shaggy's voice came from the next room. "Found it!"

"The second skull?" Blue Falcon said.

"No, even better," Shaggy said as he and Scooby entered, carrying armloads of food.

"The Falcon Fridge!" Shaggy and Scooby said at the same time.

"FYI, you are officially out of everything," Scooby added. He and Shaggy giggled.

"Yes!" Blue Falcon said, grinning. "I love these guys!" He pushed buttons on his gauntlets, summoning chairs and a table. They sat down to eat.

"All right, man," Shaggy said, setting food on the table. "Prepare your taste buds for a Scoob-Shag specialty!"

Blue Falcon saw a bowl of ice cream with a pepper on top. "Whoa. You put jalapeño peppers on your ice cream?"

"Heat and sweet!" Scooby announced.

"It's our signature dessert!" Shaggy said.

"Heat signature," Dee Dee said, thinking. "That's it!"

CHAPTER ELEVEN

"You guys are geniuses!" Dee Dee told Scooby and Shaggy.

Scooby turned to Shaggy. "You hear that? We're geniuses!"

"Take that, team-building expert," Shaggy said, tucking into the food.

Dee Dee made adjustments to her hologram of Earth. "The supernatural energy in that skull would give off a specific heat signature. All we gotta do is locate that spot!" A spot lit up on the hologram. "Boom! The skull is in the Gobi Desert!"

"BAAAANT!" Blue Falcon said, making a sound like a buzzer that tells someone their answer is wrong. He held up his phone. "Incorrect. I just found out where the skull is, and it's not in the Gobi Desert. It's in Romania!"

"Like, how do you know?" Shaggy asked with his mouth full.

Blue Falcon pointed to his phone. "I got a DM from one of my fans, who gave me the locayshe."

Dee Dee looked doubtful. "Sir, this could be a trap set by Dastardly."

Taking a bite of ice cream, Blue Falcon said, "If it was a trap, why would Anonymous use his own name?"

"Wait," Dee Dee said in disbelief. "Do you think 'Anonymous' is the name of a person?"

"Well," he said slowly, "based on your tone of voice, I don't anymore."

Dee Dee inhaled a deep breath and let it out. "Sir, we really should go to the Gobi Desert."

"I hear you," Blue Falcon said. "You make a valid point. But we're gonna do my thing, okay? To the cockpit!"

As the superhero strode decisively out of the room, Dynomutt said, "Brian, last time you listened to someone on the internet, you ended up in the hospital!"

Brian kept walking, calling back over his

shoulder, "Once they pumped the cinnamon out of me, I was fine!"

It didn't take the *Falcon Fury* long to fly to Romania. The ship landed in a spooky, deserted amusement park. Blue Falcon jumped out enthusiastically, followed much less enthusiastically by Dynomutt. Scooby and Shaggy hung back, not wanting to leave the safety of the ship.

"Hustle, you two!" Blue Falcon shouted up to them. "We haven't got all day."

Shaggy and Scooby exchanged a worried look, then followed their heroes into the creepy amusement park.

The four of them walked past booths with scruffy old stuffed animals on the shelves. These were long-abandoned prizes for carnival games, but as the friends passed by, the stuffed animals' eyes followed them. . . .

"Like, this amusement park isn't very amusing," Shaggy observed.

Blue Falcon ignored this comment. "According to my source, the second skull should be right here."

Scooby paused, noticing something. "Raggy, look!"

It was a note. Shaggy, Dynomutt, and Blue Falcon huddled around.

"It's a clue!" Blue Falcon said, excited. He read the note out loud: "'Ha, ha, ha. Look up.'"

"I told you it was a trap," Dynomutt sighed.

"We don't know that for sure," Blue Falcon insisted.

They looked up. The *Mean Machine* was passing overhead. Holding on to a dragonfly Rotten, Dick Dastardly flew out of it. "Oh, you delectably dim-witted do-gooders! You fell for my ambush!"

"Told you," Blue Falcon said smugly. "Not a trap."

BRZZZZ! A swarm of dragonfly Rottens swooped down from the *Mean Machine* to attack them.

"RUN!" Blue Falcon shouted.

"Like, that's *my* line!" Shaggy protested.

As Blue Falcon ran in one direction and Scooby and Shaggy ran in another, all pursued by Rottens, Dynomutt radioed Dee Dee for help. She flew the *Falcon Fury* within range, then began blasting the dragonfly Rottens with lasers. *ZZWAM! ZWAP! ZZHAP!*

"RETURN FIRE!" Dastardly ordered into his

wrist radio as he descended. The *Mean Machine*'s blasters began firing at Dee Dee, so she steered away to avoid being hit.

As soon as he reached the ground, Dastardly started chasing Scooby and Shaggy. "Stop right there, you filthy animal! And your dog, too!"

"This way!" Shaggy told Scooby, heading into an arcade. Once inside, they slammed the doors shut.

"Whew!" Scooby said, relieved.

The two friends noticed a Rotten peeking out of a game with holes and a whacking mallet. They rushed over and used the mallet to whack the evil robot. *WHAM! WHAM! WHAM!* They got it!

Just as they were high-fiving . . . *BOOM!* The locked door was blasted open, and Dastardly stepped through, holding his weapon.

"Whoa, dude," Shaggy said. "What do you want with us?"

"I don't care about you," Dastardly snarled to him. "You're not remotely important. It's the dog I need." He aimed his weapon and fired a blast of energy. *CHOOOM!* Shaggy was sent flying through the back wall and out of the arcade!

"RAGGY!" Scooby cried.

CHAPTER TWELVE

Shaggy sailed through the park and landed in a seat on the Ferris wheel. When he looked down, he was amazed to see Blue Falcon hiding in the same seat!

"Oh, hey," Blue Falcon said, trying to sound casual. "I know it looks like I'm hiding, but this is actually a superior vantage point!"

Back in the arcade, Scooby was terrified as Dastardly stalked toward him.

"Here, doggy," the villain said. "I've got lovely treats for you. . . ."

Panicking, Scooby ran, sliding right between Dastardly's legs.

"STAY! SIT! HEEL!" Dastardly ordered. As he

watched Scooby run off, he said, "Did nobody train this thing?"

Scooby ran through the park, and Rottens zoomed after him. He sprinted into the Hall of Mirrors!

Up in the Ferris wheel seat, Shaggy and Blue Falcon ducked as Rottens shot at them from below. *ZZAP! ZAP!*

"Brian!" Shaggy yelled. "Do something!"

"Like what?" Blue Falcon asked, searching through his utility belt for inspiration.

"Drop some Falcon bombs!" said Shaggy.

"Oh, yeah," Brian said, looking for them. "My utility belt has so many little pouches. . . ."

Shaggy pointed at one of the pouches. "They're right there!"

"Gotcha," Blue Falcon said, pulling out an energy grenade. "Twelve trillion volts, brother." He pulled the pin and offered the grenade to Shaggy. "Wanna throw it? You look like you wanna throw it."

"Do I ever!" Shaggy said, snatching the grenade. "Falcon bomb, away!"

He tossed the grenade, but it hit part of the Ferris wheel and bounced right back onto their seat. "AHHH!" both guys screamed. Shaggy picked it up and tossed it over the side. This time, the bomb dropped right into the Ferris wheel's control room.

"That's bad," Blue Falcon said.

BOOM! The grenade exploded, blowing away the Rottens, but it also sent energy crackling through the entire ride. The Ferris wheel lit up and started to spin, going so fast it broke off its base and rolled through the park with Shaggy and Blue Falcon still on it! The *Falcon Fury* zoomed down and followed the runaway ride.

In the Hall of Mirrors, Scooby was scared and alone, surrounded by Dastardly's reflection.

"Scooby Dooby Doo?" the villain said. "Where are you?"

Scooby bumped into the mirrors, trying to find a way out.

"Come, now," Dick's voice said. "Don't be scared. I love dogs. I'm a dog person. I had a dog myself once. He was an ill-tempered brute with a ghastly underbite who stank and caused me endless headaches. But he's lost now."

"Does he have a chip?" Scooby asked. "You know, one of those electronic chips?"

"Forget about him!" Dastardly snapped. "It's all about you. You, my friend, are special."

Scooby looked puzzled. "I'm not special."

"Oh, modesty," said the villain. "Listen to you. A true sign of your nobility. No, Scooby. You see, within you lies a key—"

"I don't have your key," Scooby said, realizing what Dastardly was after.

"No," Dastardly said. "You *are* the key! Join me, Scooby-Doo. I will show you how to harness your destiny and become the most important dog in the world."

"No thanks, Dastardly," Scooby said. He sniffed the air, trying to figure out where Dastardly was.

Dastardly stepped out from behind some mirrors. But when he looked around, he saw that Scooby had finally slipped out. "Drat," he growled.

Outside, the Ferris wheel was still rolling through the park with Blue Falcon and Shaggy on it, screaming, "AAAAHHHHH!"

Dastardly marched past the bumper cars. "Here, boy!" he called to Scooby. "Where are you?" To himself, he muttered, "I almost had him."

Thinking Dastardly was gone, Scooby popped his head out of a bumper car. "Phew!" he said.

But Dick jumped up behind him, triumphantly crowing, "You're mine, Scoo—"

POW! Dynomutt suddenly appeared, and pushed Dastardly back!

"Dynomutt!" Scooby cried, thrilled to see his hero. The robot-dog jumped into Scooby's bumper car, fired up two mini jet engines, and they took off! *VVWOOOM!*

Dastardly leapt into another bumper car. Rottens swarmed onto it, robotically transforming it into a speedy set of wheels for their master. Standing, Dastardly pointed and ordered, "Follow that car!" They took off so fast that Dastardly fell back into his seat.

Dynomutt and Scooby zigzagged through the park at top speed, eventually reaching the runaway Ferris wheel.

"Hey, dude!" Shaggy called to Scooby. "Like, nice wheels!"

"Thanks," Scooby said. "Look out!"

"Yikes!" Shaggy cried as the Ferris wheel crashed into a roller coaster! Blue Falcon and Shaggy were thrown off the wheel and into a roller-coaster car, which took off down the track!

"Raggy!" Scooby called, steering his jet-powered bumper car right behind it.

Dastardly followed them. "You're just making it worse for yourselves!" he shouted.

Shaggy and Blue Falcon's car crested the roller coaster, then plummeted at tremendous speed. Shaggy held on for dear life. Then he saw Blue Falcon waving his hands over his head as they descended. Shaggy let go of the bar, too . . .

. . . and flew out of the car and through the air! "AAAAAHHHHH!" he screamed.

CHAPTER THIRTEEN

THWUMP! Miraculously, Shaggy fell into Scooby and Dynomutt's bumper car. Deciding to join them, Blue Falcon jumped out of the roller-coaster car and landed right behind their car. Even with Dastardly gaining on them, Blue Falcon leapt into the bumper car, threw his arms around Shaggy and Scooby, and snapped a quick selfie.

Looking ahead, they all saw that the roller-coaster tracks were broken off from years of neglect. Dastardly climbed onto the front of his bumper car and reached toward Scooby.

"GIVE ME THAT DOG!" he yelled.

The roller-coaster car approached the broken tracks, and—*WHOOSH!* Screaming, Shaggy,

Scooby, Dynomutt, and Blue Falcon were launched into the air! But before they could fall, the *Falcon Fury* zoomed in and caught them with its blue tractor beam! As it beamed them up into the ship, Dastardly's bumper car crashed to the ground. *KA-WHAAAM!*

In the *Falcon Fury*'s cargo bay, Dee Dee rushed in as Scooby's bumper car arrived. "Welcome back, guys!" she said.

"Dastardly said I was the key!" Scooby reported.

Blue Falcon scratched Scooby behind the ears. "I knew this guy was special from the moment he set foot on my ship!" He turned to Shaggy. "What did Dastardly say about you?"

Shaggy looked away. "I believe his exact words were 'I don't care about you—you're not remotely important.' And then he called me a 'waste of space.'"

Blue Falcon frowned. "Not cool."

"And then he whooshed me through the wall," Shaggy concluded.

"Really not cool," Blue Falcon said, putting an arm around Shaggy. "But on the bright side, your friend is SUPER important! Let's get this dog a hero suit!" He rushed them out of the cargo bay and through the ship's central atrium, heading for the room that housed the suit machine. He stopped suddenly. "Oh, wait! First we need our 'before' shot!" He took a quick selfie of himself with Scooby, added a "rainbow vomit" filter (making it look as though they were puking rainbows), and posted it to his social media sites.

The photo immediately generated lots of likes and heart emojis!

"People love this dog!" Blue Falcon announced.

"Always have," Scooby said.

Dynomutt walked off in a jealous huff, murmuring, "If anyone needs me, I'll be tracking down the third skull of Cerberus." Dee Dee followed him.

🐾 🐾 🐾 🐾

Back in the amusement park, Dastardly climbed out of a hole shaped like his crashed bumper car.

"Drat, drat, double drat!" He flipped on his wrist communicator and said, "Activate my contingency plan."

In the *Mean Machine,* a broken Rotten's eyes blinked on. . . .

🐾 🐾 🐾 🐾

Scooby stood on a rotating platform in the *Falcon Fury*'s suit pod as an imaging laser measured his body. Shaggy and Blue Falcon looked on.

FSHHHT! Robotic arms sprayed Scooby with a foam that quickly hardened into the panels of his new suit. But when they reached his neck, the robots stopped and an alarm sounded. *DUH-WEET! DUH-WEET! DUH-WEET!*

"Like, what's wrong?" Shaggy asked.

Blue Falcon peered at Scooby. "Looks like that old collar is in the way of the chest panel."

Scooby looked down at the collar Shaggy had given him all those years before. He looked at Shaggy, who gave him a small nod. Reluctantly, Scooby took off his collar, and a robotic arm snatched it away from him. Then robotic arms applied the final pieces of his uniform. Another arm held up a mirror for Scooby. He liked what he saw.

"Whoa. Awesome!" he said.

"Next year, *every* dog is gonna wear this costume!" Blue Falcon enthused.

"What do you think, Raggy?" Scooby asked.

Forcing a smile, Shaggy said, "Looks great."

And then he walked away.

CHAPTER FOURTEEN

That night, Fred drove the Mystery Machine with Daphne and Velma riding along. They all missed Shaggy and Scooby.

DING! Velma got an alert on her phone. She looked at it, and was amazed to see the selfie Blue Falcon had taken with Scooby. Because of the filter Brian had used, it looked like the two of them were puking rainbows.

"Jinkies!" Velma said. "Scooby and Shaggy are with Falcon Force!" She showed her phone to Daphne and Fred.

"What?" Fred exclaimed.

"I'm so happy they're okay," Daphne said.

DWOOOOT! DWOOOOT! DWOOOOT!
A police siren blared behind them.

"Uh-oh," Velma said. Fred looked in the rearview mirror and saw a highway patrol car.

"Pull over!" the cop ordered over his loudspeaker.

"Oh, boy," Fred sighed, pulling over to the curb and parking. He turned to Velma and Daphne. "Okay, guys. Let me do the talking. My dad's best friend is a sheriff, so I know exactly what to say."

The police officer walked up to the driver's window.

Fred lowered it and said, "Good evening, officer." Then he got a good look at the cop.

She was gorgeous!

Fred stared at her, dumbstruck.

"Fred, say something!" Daphne whispered.

"Hi," Fred said.

"Do you kids have any idea how fast you were going?" the cop asked.

Daphne decided to take over. "Funny story, officer. We were rushing to capture this evil villain who we thought was trying to kill our friends—"

"Uh-huh," the cop said, cutting her off. "Step out of the vehicle. All of you."

The three got out of the van and stood across from the police officer. "You've got to believe us, officer," Fred said. "This guy is really dangerous."

"Ooh, dangerous," the cop said sarcastically. "Sounds like he's, what—a handsome guy?"

"Oh, no, no," Daphne said firmly. "Bulbous nose. Huge chin."

"But in a cool way?" the cop suggested.

"No," Daphne said. "Super gross way."

"Textbook creeper face," Velma added.

"How dare you!" the cop said, ripping off her mask. It was Dastardly!

He pressed a button on his key remote, popping open the squad car's trunk. Rottens swarmed out and restrained Fred, Velma, and Daphne.

"You have the right to remain silent," Dastardly instructed them. "And everything you said about my face will be used against you . . . in a court of *claw*!"

CLANG! A giant metal claw fastened onto the Mystery Machine and hoisted it into the sky. In their dragonfly form, the Rottens flew after the van, carrying Fred, Daphne, and Velma up and into the *Mean Machine*.

"AAAHHHH!" the friends screamed.

Looking up into the night sky and watching them go, Dastardly chuckled evilly.

In the *Falcon Fury*'s lab, Dee Dee and Dynomutt studied a holographic globe. Wearing his new suit, Scooby watched them work.

"My satellite triangulation is picking up the location of the final Cerberus skull somewhere in the Arctic," Dee Dee said.

"But the signal is too weak to get exact coordinates," Dynomutt observed.

Shaggy stood by himself at the edge of the lab. Blue Falcon slid in next to him in his moving chair.

"Hey," he said.

"Hey, man," Shaggy answered flatly.

"Let's try rescanning with alternate points of triangulation," Dynomutt suggested.

"Roger that," Dee Dee agreed.

Blue Falcon pointed a thumb toward the two scientists. "These guys, with their triangulating. Cute, right?"

"I guess," Shaggy said, shrugging.

Blue Falcon considered Shaggy. "You're feeling left out. I get it. Totally natural when two buddies realize that one of them is destined for greatness and the other one is destined for . . ." He stopped himself. He'd been about to say "loserhood," but thought that might hurt Shaggy's feelings. "You know," he said lamely. "Other stuff."

CHAPTER FIFTEEN

Shaggy looked defensive. "Scooby-Doo is my best friend, and he always will be. Whatever he's destined for, I'm destined for."

Blue Falcon clapped him hard on the shoulder, which stung a little. "That's the spirit! Anyway, I got you something."

He turned to his engineer, Keith, who handed Brian a gift basket. He passed it on to Shaggy.

"My Blue Falcon Confidence Pack. Retails for ninety-nine ninety-five," said Brian. "You got your Blue Falcon nutrition guide, Blue Falcon resistance bands, and a copy of my dad's autobiography."

Shaggy looked through the items in the basket.

"Aww, thanks, man," he said. "Means a lot coming from you."

Blue Falcon looked confused. "How do you mean?"

"Well, you know," Shaggy explained. "We both struggle with confidence. When Dastardly attacked in the amusement park, we were both freaking out and hiding—"

"Hey!" Blue Falcon interrupted. "It was a *superior vantage point*!"

Shaggy ignored him. "But, like, your father was this great hero, right?" he said. "So, like, you're expected to be one, too. Those are big shoes to fill! The pressure is monumental. Not to mention the imposter syndrome that comes with the territory. How do you breathe under the weight of all that?"

Blue Falcon stared at him. How had Shaggy figured everything out?

"Um . . . ," he said. Then he slid his chair away and left the lab.

🐾 🐾 🐾 🐾

In the *Mean Machine*, the Rottens had locked Daphne, Velma, and Fred in a cell. Velma was using a bobby pin to pick the lock.

SNAP! The pin broke.

She sighed. "There goes my last bobby pin."

Daphne moved from chair to chair in the cell, leaning back against the walls. Velma watched her.

"What are you doing, Daphne?" she asked.

"If Scooby and Shaggy were here," she explained, "they would accidentally sit on a rigged chair or bump their heads against a wall, and it would open a secret passage out of here." She bumped her head against a wall. *THUMP!* "Ow." She rubbed the back of her head.

COUGH! COUGH! WHEEZE!

They looked and saw the Rotten with the vacuum cleaner head. He was supposed to be guarding them, but he kept breaking into coughing fits.

"Poor little thing," Daphne said.

"Uh, Daph," Velma said. "He's not on our side."

Ignoring Velma, Daphne knelt to get on the Rotten's level. "Do you need help?" she asked. "It's okay. I want to help you."

Reluctantly, the Rotten came closer.

AH-CHOO!

Daphne reached through the bars and removed the front piece of the vacuum. She emptied out the filter and snapped it back into place. "Better?"

The Rotten took a deep breath. He could breathe! He hugged Daphne through the bars.

"Aww, you're welcome," Daphne said. "Hey, do you think you could help us get out of here?"

"BEEP BOOP!" the Rotten said, nodding vigorously. He unlocked the cell.

"Cool!" Fred said as they walked out.

The little Rotten led them through the lower passages of the *Mean Machine* until they were directly under the platform where Dastardly stood. He was measuring the direction of the huge skull's beam of light and plotting a course.

"Reveal your final brother to me!" he said to the skull. "Your reunion is nigh!" He checked his compass and saw a location near the North Pole. "We have it!" he called to the Rottens. "Set a course for Messick Mountain!"

"Messick Mountain?" Velma whispered. "Sounds important."

They heard Rottens approaching. The vacuum-headed Rotten pointed to a nearby door. They hurried through it, and found their way to the ship's communication deck.

Working quietly and carefully, Velma started tapping buttons on a control panel. "I'm going to see if I can find a back door into Blue Falcon's communication system," she said. "But I have no idea what I'm hacking into. . . ."

🐾 🐾 🐾 🐾

In the *Falcon Fury*'s lab, Dee Dee and Dynomutt were still scouring the holographic globe. "I've narrowed my search down to eleven possible hot spots," Dee Dee said, "but I'm going to have to check them manually."

🐾 🐾 🐾 🐾

Back in the *Mean Machine*, Velma sparked two wires together. *ZARP!*

🐾 🐾 🐾 🐾

In the *Falcon Fury*, Dynomutt shivered. "Do you smell tangerines?" Velma's hacking was affecting him! When she touched the wires again, Dynomutt went haywire! "I . . . I . . . s-suddenly f-feel f-funky."

"Dynomutt?" Dee Dee asked, concerned at his twitching and shaking.

"I'm being haaaaacked," he managed to say as his body lost control, writhing and jolting around the room. His arms and legs shot out, and weapons popped from his body and disappeared. Then Velma's voice came out of his mouth!

"Emergency!" Velma said. "Blue Falcon. Come in, Blue Falcon! I repeat, this is an emergency!"

Dynomutt slapped himself. "I repeat, I've been hacked!"

Again Velma's voice was heard. "My name is Velma Dinkley."

"Who names their kid Velma?" Dynomutt asked.

CHAPTER SIXTEEN

"We're trying to reach our friends Scooby and Shaggy," Velma said through Dynomutt.

"I can neither confirm nor deny that!" Dynomutt said.

"We're prisoners of Dick Dastardly," Velma said urgently.

Dee Dee put her mouth close to Dynomutt's, talking straight into it, hoping Velma could hear her. "Yikes!" she cried. "Where are you?"

"I don't know," Velma admitted. "But we're heading toward a place called Messick Mountain."

Dee Dee ran over to the holographic globe and found Messick Mountain. "That's close to a possible third hot spot!"

Dynomutt shook and jerked, trying to expel Velma. "The power of science compels you!" He spun around.

"Wait!" Velma cried. "Wait! Just one more minute!"

Dynomutt slapped himself again. *WHAP!* He seemed to have returned to normal. "That was unpleasant," he said.

🐾 🐾 🐾 🐾

In the *Mean Machine,* Velma, Fred, and Daphne could hear Dee Dee's voice, but there was too much static to make out all the words. She seemed to be saying, "The skull must be there. . . ."

"Hello? Hello?" Velma said. "Where are Scooby and Shaggy?"

🐾 🐾 🐾 🐾

At that moment, Scooby was actually doing heroic poses in front of a mirror on *Falcon Fury,* checking out his new suit. Shaggy tried to hide his annoyance by burying his face in a book.

"Does this make my ears look big?" Scooby asked.

Shaggy mumbled, "Makes your ego look big."

"What did you say?"

"I said fine," Shaggy lied. "You look fine."

"It sounded like you said 'ego.'"

"Nope," Shaggy said, shaking his head. "Must be in your head." As Scooby turned back to the mirror, Shaggy mumbled, "Your giant inflated head."

Scooby turned back. "What?"

"Nothing!" Shaggy said.

From the other room, Dee Dee called, "Scooby, we need you!"

As Scooby ran out, Shaggy watched him go, frowning.

🐾 🐾 🐾 🐾

In the *Mean Machine,* Velma slammed down her tools. "We lost the signal! Hello? HELLO!"

Fred noticed something on the wall—a bunch of pictures, with red yarn connecting them. Could it be Dastardly's evil plan? "Whoa," he said. "Velma, check it."

She approached and examined the pictures. "It looks like Alexander the Great went looking for the lost treasure"—she moved to another one—"and used the paw of his dog, Peritas, to open the gates to the underworld."

Fred followed one of the red pieces of yarn with his finger. "And this weirdo family tree thing connects that dog Peritas to his last living relative—Scooby-Doo?"

Velma looked at Fred. "Maybe that's why Dastardly wants him. He must think that Scooby can help him open the gates."

Fred noticed another picture. "Whoa," he said, pointing. "Who is that?"

The picture showed a huge terrifying dog attacking people.

"Cerberus," Velma said. "He was the guardian of the gates."

On the other side of the room, Daphne found a dog blanket, a chew toy, and a dog bowl, all carefully arranged and displayed. She picked up the dog bowl and read the name on the side. "Muttley?"

"Put that down!" snarled Dastardly, entering the room.

While the villain wasn't looking, Fred quickly grabbed a picture of the gate to the underworld and put it in his pocket. He wanted to be able to recognize the gate if it appeared during their search.

Rottens swarmed Fred, Velma, and Daphne.

Dastardly snatched the dog bowl from Daphne and put it back in its place.

"You have no right to be in here, Mystery Morons!" he barked.

"It's Mystery *Inc.*," Fred corrected him.

"Yeah, Fred," Velma said. "He knows."

"What happened to Muttley?" Daphne asked.

A pained expression flashed across Dastardly's face. "Muttley is gone," he said. "Forgotten. I never even think about him."

"But you kept his room and all his stuff?" Daphne pointed out.

"I've been busy," Dastardly claimed. "You know, with the collecting skulls and whatnot."

Daphne saw through him immediately. "Muttley wasn't just your dog," she said. "He was your friend."

Dastardly shook his head. "Friend? No. Muttley was my partner. My co-conspirator. Until . . ." He stood there a moment, lost in thought, remembering. He pictured himself and Muttley peering through a supernatural portal at the gold that had belonged to Alexander the Great.

"We found a once-in-a-lifetime score," he said. "A glowing gold vision. I tried to convince him to let me be the one to go. But Muttley could never turn down a shortcut. I pleaded with him—'Muttley, please don't do this!' But as usual, that flatulent fleabag wouldn't listen to reason."

He remembered exactly what had happened. Muttley had run through the portal and grabbed the treasure. But a shadow, growling in the darkness, had come up behind him, and the portal had closed.

Dastardly didn't tell them that. He just said, "He mucked it up. I left with nothing."

CHAPTER SEVENTEEN

"Return the ladies to their cell!" Dastardly told his Rottens. "The big guy stays with me."

Rottens pulled Velma and Daphne toward the door. More of them held Fred.

"Hey, let go!" Fred protested.

"Fred!" Daphne cried. She called to Dastardly from outside the door. "What are you doing with him!"

Dastardly smiled wickedly. "Oh, I have grand plans for Freddie boy."

CLANG! The heavy steel door slammed shut.

🐾 🐾 🐾 🐾

Dee Dee piloted the *Falcon Fury* over the Arctic as Dynomutt navigated. Blue Falcon and Scooby stood nearby, watching. "I'm picking up the skull's signature," Dee Dee said. "It's coming from deep inside that geothermal vent."

Though the cockpit window, they could see a steaming crevice in the snow at the base of a huge mountain.

"Locking on," Dynomutt said, "but that entry point is super squeezy. You sure you got this?"

"You should see me parallel park," Dee Dee said confidently.

Shaggy entered the cockpit just in time to hear Blue Falcon tell Scooby, "These suits are incredible, right?"

"I love them!" Scooby agreed.

"I wanna see cheeks to seats, people!" Dee Dee ordered.

"What?" Shaggy said, confused.

"Straps activated," Dee Dee said. Automatic seatbelts whipped out of the chairs and tightened around everyone except Shaggy, who hadn't sat down yet.

"Whoa!" Shaggy said. "Hey, hold up—"

"Here we go!" Dee Dee announced as she steered the ship sharply down toward the crevice.

Shaggy went flying. "AAAAAHHHH!"

The *Falcon Fury* dove into the icy crevice, barely fitting into the narrow opening. Suddenly, a huge wall of ice loomed in front of them!

"Dee Dee," Dynomutt said. "I advise we—"

"PUNCH IT!" Dee Dee said, slamming the throttle forward. *FROOOM!* Afterburners ignited, and the ship pierced right through the giant ice wall and into an amazing underground world. "Whoa. . . ." Dee Dee was astonished.

They were flying over a lush, hazy jungle. "Fascinating microclimate," Dynomutt observed. "I've never seen anything like it."

"The heat from the geothermal vents is creating a unique ecosystem," Dee Dee said. A pterodactyl flew by the window. "Which appears to be Mesozoic!" She was thrilled.

The prehistoric creature made eye contact with Scooby. "Whoa," Scooby said.

"Our instruments are going haywire down here," Dynomutt reported, looking at the control panel.

"Can you lock on to the skull's location?" Dee Dee asked.

"I don't think so," Dynomutt said. "Our tech seems to be on the fritz."

Dee Dee made a decision. "Well, then, we'll just have to go look for it on foot."

"On f-foot?" Shaggy stammered, scared at the thought of going out into this weird underground world.

Dee Dee landed the *Falcon Fury* on a sandy beach and lowered the ship's ramp. Blue Falcon, Dynomutt, and Dee Dee headed down the ramp and into the jungle. Shaggy and Scooby stood at the top of the ramp, still inside the ship. "What are we doing here?" Shaggy called to Dee Dee. "We need to help Fred, Velma, and Daphne! They're, like, prisoners!"

"The best way to help them is to make sure Dastardly doesn't get the last skull," Dee Dee called up to him.

"Okay," Shaggy said hesitantly. "But, like, what if they call back? Shouldn't someone at least stay with the ship?"

"So you wanna stay here while we venture into the dangerous jungle?" Dee Dee asked accusingly.

One day, a boy named Norville—you can call him Shaggy—
goes to the beach. No one joins his picnic.

A stray puppy without a name wants to share Shaggy's sandwich.

Shaggy names the puppy Scooby after some tasty treats.
Shaggy calls him Scoob.

Shaggy and Scoob become best friends.

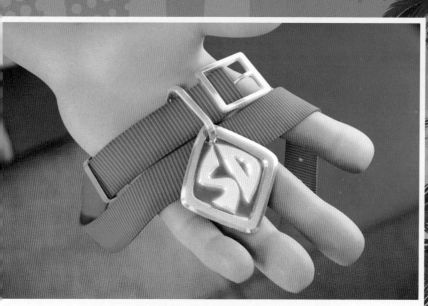

Shaggy even gives the puppy a special collar.
Scoob promises to wear it forever.

One Halloween, Shaggy and Scoob meet Fred, Velma, and Daphne.

The new friends investigate a spooky house.

Ghosts aren't real . . . are they?

Shaggy and Scoob sure believe in ghosts!

The team's adventures take them aboard a villain's airship!

They meet strange little robots.

The little robots can turn into big robots!

No matter what happens, Shaggy and Scoob stay side by side!

As long as they're together, Shaggy and Scoob can take on any foe . . .
and devour any meal.

"Uh, yeah," Shaggy said. "Scooby and I will stay, then."

"No," Dynomutt said firmly. "Scooby-Doo is coming with us."

Shaggy stepped defiantly in front of Scooby. "Scooby and I stick together. Always have, always will. Tell 'em—"

But Scooby was already headed down the ramp to join Falcon Force.

"Scoob?" Shaggy said.

CHAPTER EIGHTEEN

Scooby-Doo looked back up the ramp at Shaggy, beckoning with his paw. "Let's go with them."

"What?" Shaggy said, taken by surprise.

"Scoob's clearly important to whatever Dastardly's got planned," Dee Dee said. "We need him."

Wagging his tail proudly, Scooby said, "Yeah, I'm the key."

Shaggy just shook his head. "Who *are* you? First you whip off your collar, and now you're, what, some kind of a superhero?"

"My collar?" Scooby asked, confused.

"You promised you'd never take it off," Shaggy reminded him.

"You gave me the nod," Scooby countered.

"Yeah," Shaggy admitted, "but I didn't think you'd really do it!"

Extending his neck, Dynomutt butted into their conversation. "We really need to go."

"Just come with us," Scooby urged Shaggy.

"*Us?* You're an *us* now?" Shaggy asked. "What happened to US us?"

"Raggy . . . ," Scooby pleaded.

Shaggy folded his arms across his chest. "You need to choose. I'm staying on the ship. Are you staying with me, or going with them?"

"That isn't fair," Scooby said.

"Choose," Shaggy insisted.

Scooby looked at Shaggy, thinking. Then he turned and walked down the ramp to Falcon Force.

"Good," Shaggy said bitterly. "Who needs ya." He stormed back into the ship.

🐾 🐾 🐾 🐾

As Falcon Force made its way through the jungle, Dee Dee tried to locate the skull with a hologram device. "This still isn't working. Dyno, any luck?"

Dynomutt lit up his eyes. He scanned the area but came up empty. "I got nothing."

Pointing at Scooby, Brian said, "Who needs your techno malarky when we got this guy? Let's let a *real* dog sniff out this bone!"

Pleased by Brian's faith in him, Scooby put his nose to the ground. *SNIFF! SNIFF!* "Got it!" he announced, following the scent trail. Blue Falcon was right behind him.

He looked back at Dee Dee and Dynomutt and said, "Try and keep up with us." He hopped over a log. "Oh, yeah!"

Dee Dee looked at Dynomutt, unimpressed. "Should we follow them?"

"Unless that dog is looking for a taco truck," Dynomutt said, "he doesn't have a prayer."

SNIFF! SNIFF! Scooby kept smelling the ground, hurrying along, until he bumped into something . . . a pair of huge, hairy feet!

"Brian!" Scooby called back.

Blue Falcon ran up. "Did you find somethiiiiing?" His question turned into a yell as he was pulled up into the trees. *WHOOSH!*

Terrified, Scooby looked up and saw a giant hairy caveman looming over him!

"Ruh-roh!" Scooby said.

96

Back in the *Falcon Fury,* Shaggy headed into the lounge, muttering to himself. "Thinks he's so special. 'I'm the key.' 'I got a hero suit.' Makes his stupid ears look huge."

On a table, Scooby's collar lay with other items that were about to be thrown out. Shaggy picked it up, feeling heartbroken at first, then angry. He shoved the collar into his pocket. "Hmph. Whatever."

He was about to sit down when he heard *HONK! HONK!*

"Huh?" Shaggy said, thinking the honk sounded familiar. He headed off to investigate.

Outside, he saw . . . the Mystery Machine! And climbing out of the driver's seat . . .

"Fred?" Shaggy said. He ran toward his friend.

"Shaggy!" Fred cried, opening his arms wide.

They hugged. "Boy, am I happy to see you!" Shaggy said. "Wait, how did you get here? Where are Daphne and Velma?"

"Dastardly kidnapped us and was holding us captive on his super-awesome airship," Fred said. He looked around. "Where's Scooby?"

Shaggy crossed his arms and looked annoyed. "He's got a new gang now."

"Scooby is in danger," Fred said. "Dastardly's on his way here, and he won't stop until he gets the key."

"Ugh," Shaggy groaned. "I am so over him."

"What're you talking about?" Fred asked.

Shaggy gave Fred a quick look, but said, "He's with his hero friends, looking for that stupid skull."

"Listen, Shaggy," Fred said, "those pseudo supers can't protect him like you can. You guys are best friends. I wish I had a friendship like that!"

Shaggy sighed, convinced. "Yeah, okay."

"Now take me to Scooby," Fred said.

🐾 🐾 🐾 🐾

At that moment, Scooby and Blue Falcon were tied to a tall stone column in a large arena with a throne in it. They were surrounded by giant cavepeople.

Looking scared, Scooby struggled to break free. "Brian, where are we? What do we do?"

High in the arena, two figures emerged from the shadows—Dynomutt and Dee Dee. They looked down at Scooby and Blue Falcon, tied to the column.

"There's our boy," Dynomutt whispered. He sighed. "When I promised his father I would look after him, I never dreamed it would be this much work."

TA-RAAAH! A horn blew, and the cavepeople started to stomp their massive feet. *THUMP! THUMP! THUMP! THUMP!* They all looked expectantly toward the gate at the end of the arena.

The gate swung open, and four giant cavepeople marched into the arena, carrying a platform. On the platform was the third skull, decorated with flowers, vines, and glowing torches.

"Look!" Dee Dee said, pointing. "It's the skull! Come on!"

Blue Falcon and Scooby stared at the approaching skull. Horns blew and drums beat a wild rhythm. The jaws of the skull slowly opened. Then a voice came from it. . . .

"Hello, cavepersons! What delights have you brought me today?"

"Ruh-roh!" Scooby said.

Extending his talons, Blue Falcon started sawing away at the vines that held them.

A tiny caveman jumped out of the mouth of the skull. "Hello!" he said.

"This one doesn't look so tough," Blue Falcon said to Scooby.

The little caveman walked up to Blue Falcon and Scooby, admiring their outfits. "Wow!" he said. "So bright and shiny!" He looked into the crowd of giant cavepeople. "Nice work, Carl!" he called to one of them. "You get extra worms in your food today." Carl patted his heart to show his thanks.

"Stand back!" Blue Falcon said in his most intimidating voice. "I'm . . . BLUE FALCON!"

The crowd went silent.

"Holy skull!" the little caveman said. "You speak?" He was obviously shocked.

"Of course we speak!" Scooby said. "*You* speak."

"But I'm the only one around here who does. You don't know how happy I am to see you!" the caveman said, smiling.

"You are?" Scooby said.

"Yeah, dog, I got no one to talk to," the little caveman said. "Basically, I'm the king because I'm the first guy to string two words together. And until you showed up, the last!"

"So talking made you king?" Blue Falcon asked, amazed.

The short king spread his thick arms open wide. "I'm evolution in action, baby!"

"Well, Mister King," Scooby said respectfully, "we just need to take your skull and go."

The caveman's smile disappeared. "Go? I finally find someone I can share my hopes and dreams with, and you want to leave?" He stared at Scooby intensely. "You must stay here . . . forever!"

"Forever?" Scooby yelped. "But my friends are in trouble!"

Blue Falcon was still cutting through the vines. "Don't worry," he whispered to Scooby. "I got this." *SNAP!* He broke his tethers and leapt forward. "Listen, little man—"

The crowd went silent again.

"Little?" the king said. "Did you just call me little?"

"No," Scooby lied. "He said big."

Blue Falcon had no interest in lying. "I did call you little. Pipsqueak."

The crowd of cavepeople grew agitated. Carl started to move forward, ready to protect his king.

"No, no, Carl," the little caveman said. "I don't need help."

As the members of the crowd stomped their feet, the king and Blue Falcon circled each other, bobbing and weaving like boxers in a ring, sizing each other up.

Moving closer to the arena floor, Dynomutt and Dee Dee saw Blue Falcon and the caveman king squaring off.

"Oh, no," Dynomutt said. "Brian's starting to improvise."

"You make a break for the skull," Dee Dee instructed, "and I'll go pick up Brian and Scooby."

"Sounds like a plan," Dynomutt agreed.

Screaming "AAAHHH!" Blue Falcon lunged at the king fist-first. The little caveman stepped aside, bashing Brian with his club as he went sailing by. *WHAM!* Blue Falcon smashed through a wall. *CRASH!*

The crowd cheered!

"I love a challenge like I love dinosaur eggs: over easy," the king gloated.

Dee Dee jumped down into the arena and sprang into action, crying, "Leave him alone!"

"More friends!" the king said, delighted. "Let's stay up late and braid each other's armpit hair!"

Swinging a pipe, Dee Dee attacked the tiny caveman, but he easily dodged her blows.

"Too slow!" he said. But just as he was about to counterattack . . . *HONK! HONK!*

The Mystery Machine blasted through the arena gates! *KERRAAASH!*

The caveman king marveled at the sight of the vehicle. "Dang, those are some dope wheels!" *BZZOYYT!* Seeing that the caveman was distracted, Dynomutt fired a blast that sent the king flying through the arena wall. His voice came through the hole his body had made: "Whatever wheels are."

Shaggy jumped out of the van and ran to Scooby. "Scooby! Dastardly's on his way!"

"Raggy!" Scooby said, astonished to see his friend.

"Hurry!" Shaggy urged. "We have to get out of here!"

"Where did that van come from?" Dynomutt asked.

Fred stepped out of it.

"We're in danger," Shaggy said. "Tell 'em, Fred."

"Tell them what?" Fred asked, throwing a friendly arm around Shaggy. "How you led me here? Or, more specifically, how you led me to the third skull . . ."

"Wait, what are you—" Shaggy started to ask, bewildered.

"...*and* Scooby-Doo?" Fred finished, squeezing Shaggy.

"You're hurting me!" Shaggy said.

"Fred, why are you doing this?" Scooby asked.

"I have a treasure to collect," Fred explained. He flashed an evil grin, then ripped off his mask to reveal . . . DICK DASTARDLY! Laughing, Dastardly held his sprayer to Shaggy's head!

CHAPTER NINETEEN

"Dick Dastardly!" Blue Falcon, Dynomutt, and Dee Dee said at the same time. Blue Falcon started to run toward the villain, but Dastardly pushed his sprayer against Shaggy's temple.

"Uh-uh-uh," Dastardly warned. "I wouldn't come any closer."

"Raggy . . . ," Scooby said, worried about his friend.

Dee Dee got down to business. "What do you want, Dastardly?" She had a pretty good idea she already knew the answer.

"Give me Scooby or the hippie gets gooped," Dastardly said.

Shaggy looked straight at Scooby. "You don't have to do this, Scoob."

"Enough!" Dastardly said impatiently. "Three seconds! One . . . two . . ."

"Let him go," Scooby growled. He marched forward, willing to hand himself over to Dastardly to save his friend.

"Scooby, no!" Shaggy cried.

Dastardly grinned. "Good boy," he told Scooby, pushing Shaggy aside and grabbing the Great Dane. As the *Mean Machine* zoomed in, Dastardly laughed triumphantly.

At the sight of the flying ship, the cavepeople fled in panic.

The *Mean Machine* lowered its claw and grabbed ahold of the skull. Dragonfly Rottens swarmed into the arena, panicking the cavepeople even more. Dastardly hopped onto the claw, dragging Scooby with him. They rode the claw up into the *Mean Machine*.

"Oh, I almost forgot to take out the rubbish," Dastardly said, snickering. A Rotten brought Fred, Velma, and Daphne, bound and gagged, out to the edge of the ramp that led into the ship. Then Dastardly shoved them off the ship!

"MPHFF!" they screamed through their gags.

Dynomutt and Dee Dee leapt into action. Dynomutt caught Velma, and Dee Dee caught Daphne.

"Wow!" Blue Falcon said. "Nice catch, guys!" He gave them two thumbs up, just in time for Fred to fall into his arms.

"Ta-ta!" Dastardly called from the *Mean Machine*. "See you all in Athens!" Then he laughed. "No, you won't! Because the only way out is with a jet!"

"Good thing we have one!" Blue Falcon called back.

"Oh, do you, now?" Dastardly asked ominously. "Mwah-ha-ha-ha-ha-ha-ha!" The *Mean Machine* zoomed off, heading for the crevice that led back to the surface.

"Raggy!" Scooby called as they flew away.

"Scooby!" Shaggy called back.

Shaggy, Dee Dee, Dynomutt, Fred, Velma, and Daphne looked worried.

Blue Falcon said, "There's something about the way he said 'do you' and then laughed that makes me think he did something to our ship. . . ."

When they got back to the *Falcon Fury,* they found that Dastardly had blown the wings off. Then—

CRASH! The body of the jet fell off its falcon legs.

"Yes!" Blue Falcon exclaimed, pumping a fist. "I was right! He *did* do something to our ship."

"You really think that's worthy of celebration?" Dynomutt asked.

"I don't get a lot of wins," Blue Falcon admitted.

Upset, Dee Dee examined the wreckage. "The primary engine's destroyed!" she groaned. "The thrusters are intact, but they're too small to launch the ship."

"So, we're stuck here?" Blue Falcon said. He pointed at Shaggy. "Well, maybe if your little buddy didn't lead the bad guy right to us . . ."

Fred stepped between Blue Falcon and Shaggy and pushed Brian away. "Hey, leave Shaggy alone."

"Yeah," Velma said to Blue Falcon, "what kind of a hero blames other people for his problems?"

"Meet Brian," Dynomutt said dryly.

"Hey!" Brian said, turning on Dynomutt. "You shut your dog face!"

"You know, none of us would be here if you hadn't stolen our friends in the first place!" Daphne pointed out.

Dee Dee stepped in. "Whoa, we *saved* your friends from Dastardly!"

"Some saving!" Fred said. He pointed a finger at Blue Falcon. "Scooby-Doo has a first-class ticket to the apocalypse!"

Blue Falcon pointed two fingers at Fred. "Don't you point at me!"

"Don't you double-point at me!" Fred yelled back.

"Don't single-point at me!" Blue Falcon shouted.

They started shoving each other. "I'll point at whoever I want to point at!" Fred said.

Dee Dee, Daphne, and Velma tried to break them apart. Dynomutt tugged on Brian's cape.

"Hey, get off him!" Daphne yelled.

"He's the one that started it!" Dee Dee shouted.

"Let him go!" Daphne insisted.

"Guys, enough with the pointing and shoving!" Velma said.

Shaggy climbed atop a boulder and threw his arms in the air. "STOP! STOP IT, ALL OF YOU!"

They stopped fighting and stared at Shaggy.

"Oh, wow," Shaggy said. "That worked." He stood on the rock with his arms still in the air. "And now you're all staring at me."

"Well?" Blue Falcon asked. "Are you going to say something?"

"Um . . . yeah," Shaggy said, lowering his arms.

"You know when you're making a sandwich . . ."

"Oh, boy," Fred sighed.

". . . and at first none of the ingredients seem like they go together? Roasted peppers and lime juice. Horseradish and plantains. Smoked turkey and—"

"Um, Shaggy," Velma interrupted, sensing that he was straying off topic.

"The point is," Shaggy said, climbing off the rock, "sometimes the best sandwiches come from the most unlikely and rando ingredients. And that's what we are." He looked around at the others. "A bunch of rando people thrown together. But if can work with one another like a team, then we can turn this soggy sandwich into . . . a *hero* sandwich!"

Surprised to find themselves inspired by Shaggy's speech, the others smiled at each other.

"So what do you say we save Scooby-Doo?" Shaggy asked. "Who's with me?"

They all cheered.

"Woo-hoo!" Shaggy shouted. "Let's do this!"

CHAPTER TWENTY

Working together, the members of Mystery Falcon Inc. Force used parts from the *Falcon Fury* to convert the Mystery Machine van into a flying craft. When the work was finished, they all squeezed inside, and Fred took the wheel.

"All right!" he said. "Let's see if this thing's got legs."

It did, since they'd added the legs from the *Falcon Fury*. But the remodeled vehicle didn't know how to use them. It stumbled, and the legs tripped into the splits. The body slammed to the ground. *KLUNK!*

"Come on!" Fred urged, maneuvering the controls. He finally got the vehicle walking. The engines on the sides came to life and ignited with flames. *WHOOSH!* "Nothing to it!" Fred pulled a lever and they lifted off, climbing into the air!

🐾 🐾 🐾 🐾

In Athens, tourists were happily visiting the ancient ruins of the Acropolis. Suddenly, a shadow passed over them. They looked up and saw the gigantic *Mean Machine*. A hatch opened, and Rottens began to lower the three huge, leering skulls. Screaming, the tourists fled.

Scooby watched from the airship. "You won't get away with this!" he told Dastardly.

"Why do people always say that?" the villain responded. "Because I am quite literally getting away with it. The only thing spoiling this moment is your ridiculous suit." He turned to the Rottens and snapped his fingers with an order: "Take it off!"

The robots swarmed over Scooby, ripping off his hero suit.

Holding Scooby on a chain, Dastardly rode the claw down to the Acropolis. The three skulls fit perfectly into designated spots on the ruined structure. When the third skull was in place, they all began to glow. A green mist poured out of the skulls' mouths and wrapped around the ruins. The Acropolis immediately rebuilt itself—the city was restored to its former ancient glory!

"How long have I been waiting for this very moment!" Dastardly cried.

The green mist parted, revealing massive carved gates. As green lightning crackled around them, the gates swung open, revealing a magic portal with a lock shaped like a dog's paw.

"Give me your paw!" Dastardly ordered Scooby.

"No!" Scooby said, drawing back.

BEEP! BEEP! An alarm on the villain's watch was alerting him to an incoming danger.

"What?" Dastardly said. He looked at his watch and saw the Mystery Machine flying toward them. "I thought you meddling millennials were gone for good!" He turned to his Rottens. "DESTROY THOSE FALCON FOOLS!"

BOOM! The Rottens fired a rocket right at the Mystery Machine! It smashed into the flying van's wing, sending it plunging toward the earth. Everyone inside screamed!

"WE'RE ALL GONNA DIE!" they cried.

But Dynomutt hustled out of the van, ignited his

booster rockets, and flew around the plummeting Mystery Machine. *FWOOMPH!* His rockets flared at full power. Then . . .

SPLAT! Dynomutt collided with the windshield. Using his rockets, he managed to slow the van's fall, though it was still a rough landing. *WHOMP!*

🐾 🐾 🐾 🐾

Back at the huge gates, Dastardly pressed Scooby's paw against the lock. The magical portal glowed, and slowly opened.

"It's happening!" Dastardly cried. "It's finally happening! And now to fetch my treasure!" He walked through the portal and into the darkness. Scooby hid behind the open gate.

🐾 🐾 🐾 🐾

Dynomutt pried the dented doors of the Mystery Machine open. Dee Dee, Blue Falcon, Fred, Velma, and Daphne spilled out, lucky to be alive.

"Everybody okay?" Daphne asked.

★ ★ ★ ★

Inside Dastardly's *Mean Machine,* the little Rotten with the vacuum cleaner head saw on a screen that Daphne was alive. He did a happy dance! But then he saw the open gate to the underworld. The Rotten got a determined look. . . .

★ ★ ★ ★

"We gotta get to Scooby!" Daphne told the others.

"Wait!" Fred said, staring at the wrecked van. He retrieved an old gym bag from the Mystery Machine seconds before it burst into flame. *BOOOOOM!* Burning pieces flew off and they all ducked.

CHAPTER TWENTY-ONE

Daphne and Velma looked at the van's scattered remains. Daphne found a whistle, and Velma grabbed a fire extinguisher. They followed Fred up the stairs.

"We're coming for you, Scoob!" Shaggy yelled.

Up by the gates, Scooby spotted them coming. He ran out from his hiding spot. "Raggy!"

🐾 🐾 🐾 🐾

Dick Dastardly had passed through the magical portal and into the underworld. He wandered for a few moments, then climbed a hill. When he reached the top, he peered down into a pit and saw it: the treasure!

"The lost treasure!" he gasped. "I've imagined this moment for so long, pondering what I would do." He dove into the shiny pile of gold and jewels like he was jumping into a swimming pool. "CANNONBALL!"

Surrounded by treasure, he tossed gold into the air and laughed triumphantly.

At the Acropolis, Shaggy rushed through an opening to reach Scooby. They hugged.

"Buddy!" Shaggy cried.

"You're alive!" Scooby exclaimed, thrilled to be reunited with his friend.

Dastardly lay on top of the treasure trove, moving his arms and legs, making treasure angels. He filled his pockets, donned a crown, draped strands of pearls around his neck, and slid rings onto every finger.

"I've done it!" he crowed. "Unimaginable wealth! Oh, Muttley, if you could see me now!"

A shadow ran by.

"Muttley?"

The shadow passed again.

"MUTTLEY?"

Silence.

"Muttley, is that you?" Dastardly called out. "I was coming to find you next! Honest! Now, get out here." Standing next to a gold statue, Dastardly searched for whoever had cast the fleeting shadow.

WHAP! Muttley jumped down from the statue and tackled Dastardly. "Sassa-frass, shuttem up!" he hissed, raising a paw to his face to make a shushing gesture.

Dastardly was thrilled to see his old pal. "Oh, Muttley, you mangy mouth-breather! How I've missed you!"

Muttley clamped his paw over Dastardly's mouth to keep him quiet.

But it was too late. He'd already been heard.

As Dastardly watched, horrified, a huge head rose into view.

"Drat," Dastardly managed to say.

Another head rose.

"Double drat," he said.

And then a third head rose. Dastardly and Muttley were terrified.

"Triple drat," Dastardly squeaked.

Finally, the whole gang reached the massive gates. *RRRUUUMMBLE!* The ground shook!

"Uh, what was that?" Blue Falcon asked.

"Something's coming!" Daphne exclaimed.

"We gotta close these gates!" Scooby said.

Summoning all their strength, they slowly pushed the two gates toward each other. In the gap between the gates, lightning crackled, and a buzzing sound filled the air.

"We . . . can . . . do this!" Shaggy grunted.

At last, they managed to close the two gates together. *BOOM!*

"Yeah!" Fred cheered. "We did it!"

"Mission accomplished!" Blue Falcon announced, high-fiving Fred.

But Velma was studying a hieroglyphic on the gate. It showed a man and a dog pressing a hand and a paw against the lock pad.

"Wait," she said. "It's not enough to close the gates! We have to *lock* them!"

BOOM! BOOM! The ground trembled. Then the gates banged open, and Dastardly and Muttley ran through, screaming, "AAAAHHHHH!"

"Dastardly?" Velma said, surprised to see him.

The gates shook! A giant paw stepped through the gap, followed by . . .

CERBERUS, THE GIANT THREE-HEADED DOG WHO GUARDED THE UNDERWORLD!

CHAPTER TWENTY-TWO

With his huge paw, Cerberus swatted Dastardly and Muttley aside, knocking them into a pillar. Roaring, he charged Mystery Falcon Inc. Force. *RROOOAAAARRR!*

"Come on!" Velma urged the others. "Hurry! RUN!"

They ran and hid behind some stone columns. Cerberus tried to push his heads through to reach them.

"AAAH!" they screamed.

"Zoinks!" Shaggy yelled.

As the gang huddled in their hiding place, Daphne asked, "How are we going to lock magical doors from the underworld?"

"There was some kind of clue on the gates," Velma said. "I need to get back there."

"I'll get you there," Fred said bravely.

Daphne reached toward Fred. "Give me the gym bag. We'll distract Cerberus." He handed her the old gym bag he'd saved from the burning Mystery Machine.

"And the Falcon Force will provide cover," Dynomutt added.

Scooby peeked cautiously around his column and saw Cerberus about to smash it with his tail. "LOOK OUT!" Scooby screamed. *WHAM!* They dove out of the way just as Cerberus destroyed the column.

Daphne pulled ghost repellant out of the gym bag. "Time to teach an old dog a new trick!" She lobbed the canister at Cerberus, and it made a thick cloud of smoke. "Now, Velma!" she shouted.

Fred grabbed Velma's arm and they sprinted toward the gates.

Cerberus pushed through the smoke and closed in on Daphne.

"Nice doggie," she said, backing away.

🐾 🐾 🐾 🐾

Inside the *Mean Machine,* the little vacuum-headed Rotten stood in front of a horde of Rottens, watching Daphne on a screen. He could see that she was in trouble. He turned to his fellow Rottens and delivered a rousing speech: "BEEP BOOP BEEP BEEP BARP BOP BOOP!"

At the Acropolis, Cerberus had Daphne cornered. But Dynomutt readied his missiles.

"I got you!" he assured her.

BWOOM! Dynomutt fired a missile at Cerberus. Direct hit! Squealing in pain, Cerberus swatted Dynomutt, sending him crashing into a column.

"I think that just made him angrier!" Daphne cried.

Cerberus came after Daphne, but a swarm of Rottens, led by the little vacuum-headed one, attacked! *ZAP!* They blasted Cerberus—but their bursts of energy had no effect on the three-headed monster. *WHACK!* Cerberus knocked the vacuum-headed Rotten out of the sky. He landed in Daphne's arms.

"Are you okay, little guy?" she asked, concerned.

He nodded and beeped, "Yes."

"Phew!" Daphne sighed in relief. She kissed him on the cheek. The little robot blushed, covering his eyes with his hands.

As the battle raged, Dynomutt found Blue Falcon hiding behind a column.

"Brian!" Dynomutt said. "What are you doing back here?"

"It's a superior vantage point?" Blue Falcon lamely suggested.

"Get back in the game!" Dynomutt commanded.

Still wielding her high-tech staff, Dee Dee joined them. "What's going on here?"

"I hate this game," Blue Falcon admitted. "Dad made it look so . . ."

"Easy?" Dynomutt said. "It was never easy."

Scooby and Shaggy took cover, but Cerberus quickly found them.

"Zoinks!" Shaggy yelled. "Run, Scoob!"

They took off, with Cerberus right on their tails, snarling.

Dynomutt told Blue Falcon, "Your father respected his team. You're only in it for yourself!"

"Stop," Dee Dee said. "Look, I didn't know Brian's dad. But judging from the man you just described, maybe he trusted his son because he knew that deep down, he had what it takes." She turned to Dynomutt. "And maybe he knew that with you by Brian's side, teaching him the ropes, the Falcon inside was sure to find a way to soar."

Cerberus's gigantic tail swung right at their heads. They ducked.

"Help!" Shaggy cried.

Brightening, Dynomutt got an idea. "That's it! It's time for you to spread your wings and fly."

"I know," Blue Falcon said. "Dee Dee just said something really similar."

"You know you have actual wings and can fly, right?" Dynomutt asked. He pressed a button on Blue Falcon's belt. Wings shot out of his costume!

"Oh, right," Blue Falcon said. "The wings . . ." He rose triumphantly into the air, looking heroic. Then—*SPLAT!* He flew right into a wall. "Got a little too excited on the takeoff."

Cerberus trapped Scooby and Shaggy with his enormous paws. He picked them up like a cat playing with mice, dangling Scooby over one of his mouths.

"Scooby!" Shaggy cried.

The three-headed beast was about to devour Scooby like a snack!

CHAPTER TWENTY-THREE

Cerberus dropped Scooby. He fell toward the monster's huge mouth, full of razor-sharp teeth, until . . . Blue Falcon flew in and caught Scooby in his arms!

"I got you!" he cried.

Dynomutt flew in, too, rescuing Shaggy from the giant dog's grip.

Velma and Fred were trying to figure out how to lock the gates to the underworld.

"I think there's more than one key," Velma said. "Look at this carving. The man, Alexander the Great, is on one side, and the dog, Peritas, is on the other."

Fred stared at the image on the gate. "Wait, I've

seen that before!" He reached in his pocket and pulled out the picture he'd taken from Dastardly's planning room on the *Mean Machine*. "The carving on the gate looks like this picture I found on Dastardly's ship. See?"

Velma examined the picture. "'Par Nobilis,'" she read. "That means 'the noble pair.'"

While Fred and Velma tried to figure out how to lock the gate, the others continued to distract Cerberus.

"Oh, Cerberus!" Daphne called. "Here, boy!"

The beast turned one of its heads toward Daphne.

"What do you say we turn it up a notch?" Dynomutt suggested to Blue Falcon.

"You got it!" Brian agreed. The two of them flew circles around Cerberus. The ancient dog followed their flight with all six of his eyes.

Watching, Shaggy got an idea. "They got him distracted," he said. He turned to the friendly little Rotten with the vacuum-cleaner head. "Hey, little guy. Remember at the bowling alley when you transformed into that thing?"

The little Rotten turned to another Rotten.

"BEEP BOOP BORP BLEEP!" Then he changed into a fierce-looking dragonfly.

"No, no," Shaggy said, shaking his head. "Not that scary thing."

Over by Cerberus, Daphne kept trying to distract it. "Hey, hey! Over here!" she said, waving her arms.

Fred and Velma ran over to her just then.

"Guys," Velma said. "To lock the gates, we need a man and his dog. A noble pair."

"That must be Dynomutt and me," Blue Falcon said immodestly.

"No," Daphne disagreed. "It's Scooby and Shaggy."

Shaggy had gotten the little Rotten to change out of his dragonfly-form, but now he became a bowling pin. "Okay, okay," Shaggy said. "Before the creepy dragonfly, but after the scary bowling pin."

Finally, the Rotten transformed into a bowling ball.

"Yes!" Shaggy cheered. "That's it!"

Meanwhile, Velma was explaining one more requirement for locking the gates. "But there's a catch. In order to lock the gates for good, Peritas had to be on the inside."

Daphne looked worried. "Does that mean Scooby—"

"No," Fred insisted. "There has to be another way!"

Across the courtyard, Shaggy and Scooby picked up their little Rotten friend and another Rotten who had also transformed into a bowling ball. The friends hurled the balls at Cerberus—and then dozens of other Rotten bowling balls.

Cerberus slipped and scrambled, losing his balance on the rolling balls and stumbling back through the gates! Shaggy and Scooby high-fived.

"Man, that's like a mega strike!" Shaggy said.

"Perfect game," Scooby agreed.

Blue Falcon, Dynomutt, and Dee Dee shut the massive gates. *KLONK!*

"Okay," Shaggy said. "So how do we lock these puppies up?"

The others looked upset. "What?" Shaggy asked.

Velma stepped forward. "Alexander held the gates shut here . . ."

". . . while Peritas stayed behind in the underworld," Daphne concluded miserably.

Shaggy and Scooby understood exactly what this meant.

"What? No!" Shaggy said. "There has to be another way. Right, Velma?"

Velma had no answer for him.

"There is no other way," Scooby said bravely. "I'm the key. I love you, Raggy." He lifted his paw toward the lock, but—

Shaggy beat him to it! "It says one of us had to be on the inside," Shaggy said. "It doesn't say which one."

"No!" Scooby said. "Raggy!"

Each kept trying to put his paw or hand on the lock, until finally Shaggy jumped in front of it, facing Scooby.

"Scoob, I can't let you do this," he said. "You are the best friend I could ever ask for. When I'm lonely, you keep me company. When I'm scared, you make me laugh. When I'm hungry, you make me something deliciously gross that only we like."

Tears filled Scooby's eyes.

"You have been the key to the best times of my

life," Shaggy said. "Now it's my turn." He put his hand on the lock and was transported to the other side of the gates. The gates began to lock . . . for good.

"No, Raggy!" Scooby cried.

CHAPTER TWENTY-FOUR

But Scooby realized he had no choice. He placed his paw on the gate, and the portal to the underworld locked. The ground trembled, and in a giant swirl of mystical energy, the Acropolis returned to modern-day ruins. Scooby collapsed to his knees and howled. The others gathered around to comfort him, weeping. But then . . .

A magical light opened a small portal! Shaggy was tossed out of the ruins, landing on the ground.

"Zoinks, what a day!" he said.

Scooby turned and saw him. "RAGGY!"

"It spit me out!" Shaggy said.

Everyone rushed over to greet him. "But how?" Fred asked.

"I dunno," Shaggy admitted, shrugging. "But it was seriously trippy."

"The underworld rejected you," Velma said, amazed.

"Of course it did," Dynomutt said dryly.

"A mismatch of quantum energies," Dee Dee suggested.

"Because Shaggy never belonged there," Daphne concluded.

Shaggy grinned. "It's gonna take more than a three-headed monster to keep me away from my best friend!" He hugged Scooby, and the others joined in a big group hug.

BUZZZZZ! They looked up in the sky and saw the Rottens carrying Dastardly and Muttley.

"Put me down, you revolting rubbish receptacles!" Dastardly snarled. Following his orders, the Rottens dropped the two villains right at the feet of the do-gooders. *WHUMP! WHUMP!*

"Rasm-frasm robots," Muttley complained.

The Rottens landed, transforming into terrifying scorpions. They hissed at Dastardly threateningly.

"Time to pay for your crimes, Dick Dastardly!" Blue Falcon said.

"Or is it?" Shaggy asked.

Dastardly pulled off his mask, revealing . . .

"The team-building expert?" said the members of Mystery Inc., astonished.

"Wow," Daphne marveled. "That's an impressive impersonation."

"Thank you," the expert said. "I was also the lead in my high school's production of *Annie*."

"Wait a minute," Velma said. "This makes no sense. Why would that team-building expert want Muttley? And how could he do all those things, like build a giant flying *Mean Machine*?" She reached over and pulled off the expert's mask, revealing . . .

"Dick Dastardly?" they all said.

"You're coming with us," Blue Falcon said, taking him by the arm.

"I would've gotten away with it," Dastardly growled, "if it weren't for you mismatched meddling miscreants!"

Brian dragged Dastardly and Muttley away.

🐾 🐾 🐾 🐾

One morning a few weeks later, Fred, Velma, and Daphne were putting the finishing touches on their new headquarters—Mystery Inc.: Supernatural

Mystery Solvers—just in time for its grand opening.

Fred stepped back to admire the sign over the entrance. "It's perfect." He looked around. "Where are those guys?"

"Don't worry," Daphne assured him. "They'll be here."

"Maybe we should start without them," Fred said.

"I think we learned our lesson last time," Velma said.

HONK! HONK!

The three looked around, but they saw no sign of Shaggy and Scooby. Then, above them, a new Mystery Machine appeared in the sky, driven by Dee Dee and Dynomutt! It was being lowered to the ground by the *Falcon Fury*'s reverse tractor beam.

As the flying van gently landed, Scooby and Shaggy jumped out of the back. Standing on the roof, Blue Falcon spun music like a DJ. Balloons floated down from the sky. A crowd gathered to see what was going on.

"And that," Blue Falcon said, "is how you make an entrance!"

Fred walked up to the new Mystery Machine and hugged it. "I'm so happy you're back!" he said to it.

Dee Dee and Dynomutt watched Blue Falcon get

the crowd going, urging them to dance.

"He really knows how to throw a party," Dee Dee said, "and Keith even got the balloons right this time."

Keith's voice came over the *Falcon Fury*'s loudspeaker. "Thanks, Dee Dee!"

"I could use a hand looking after him," Dynomutt sighed.

"He'll get the hang of it," Dee Dee said. "I bet even his dad wasn't Blue Falcon on his first mission."

Dynomutt looked at the scientist. "You know, you should think about donning the feathers yourself one of these days."

Dee Dee shook her head. "Nah, I don't need to be Blue Falcon. I'm good being Dee Dee Skyes, one bad mamma jamma!" She and Dynomutt shared a smile.

As the grand opening party really got under way, Scooby and Shaggy scarfed down some hot dogs.

Suddenly, an announcement came over the Mystery Machine's police scanner: "All units, we have a missing person report in San Pedro. Last seen being dragged into the ocean mist by the ghost of an old sea captain."

"Gh-gh-ghost?" Scooby and Shaggy said nervously.

"Looks like we're on the case!" Velma said.

"Let's hit it!" Fred said.

Daphne stuck her head through the open door of their new place. "Hey, Dusty," she called, "watch the shop, please." Inside, the little Rotten with the vacuum-cleaner head stopped spinning on a chair.

"BLEEP BLOOP BLOOP!"

Fred, Velma, and Daphne piled into the van and beckoned for Shaggy and Scooby to join them. The two pals looked at each other.

"What do you say, buddy?" Shaggy asked.

"Let's Scooby Dooby *Doo* it!" Scoob answered.

They high-fived and jumped in the new Mystery Machine, ready for their next big adventure!

137

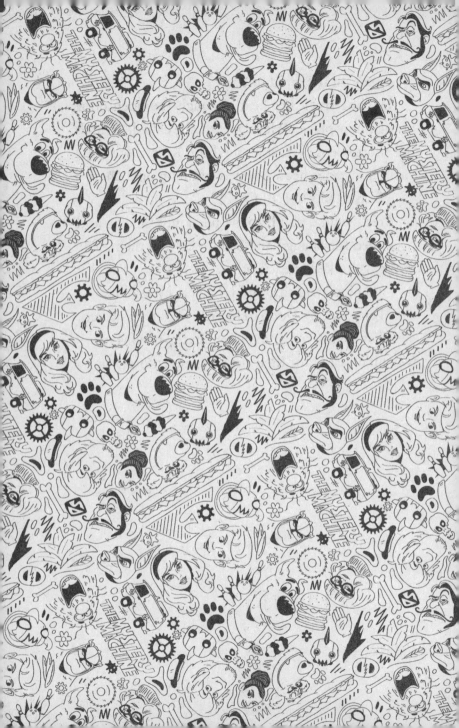

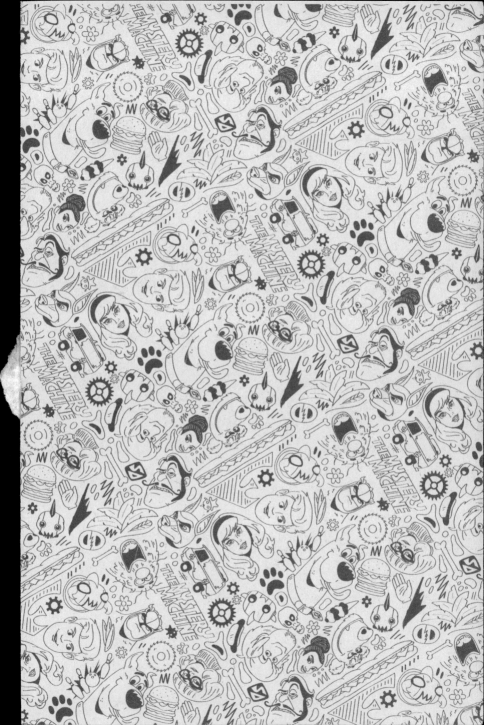